SKYLIGHTS

A STARGAZERS STORY

L.P. HERNANDEZ

SOBELO BOOKS

Book Cover by Geoff Parrell and Chris Panatier
Edited by L.C. Marino and L.P. Hernandez

Formatted and published by Sobelo Books

ISBN (paperback): 978-1-965389-24-9
ISBN (ebook): 978-1-965389-23-2

First edition, 2025

Contents

Dedication   V

Before   1

Chapter One   3

Posted by Coloradokid_14 3 days ago   23

Chapter Two   27

Apocalypse Radio   35

Chapter Three   41

Apocalypse Radio   57

Chapter Four   61

Apocalypse Radio   73

Chapter Five   77

Apocalypse Radio   91

Chapter Six   95

Apocalypse Radio   107

Chapter Seven   113

Apocalypse Radio   127

Chapter Eight 131

Apocalypse Radio 145

Chapter Nine 151

Apocalypse Radio 169

Chapter Ten 177

Chapter Eleven 195

Chapter Twelve 217

Chapter Thirteen 231

Apocalypse Radio 239

Quick Favor 241

Acknowledgements 242

About the Author 245

This novel is dedicated to everyone who asked if there would be a sequel.

Before

In short, the world came undone. It began with a forum post titled *My Neighbor Has Been Staring at the Moon for Hours*, the first documented report of a *Stargazer*, as they would come to be known. Each night there were more; family members and neighbors turned to sentinels, faces aimed at the night sky. In the morning, they had changed. They were Stargazers—mindless murderers, destroyers, and drifters.

The Sylva family planned their escape, joining the dwindling number of non-Stargazers fleeing the city. The night was polluted with gunfire, screams, and screeching tires. Penny, almost five-years-old, slept through it all. Exhausted, her parents eventually did as well, only for Henry to wake and discover the open front door. Judith stood outside, staring at the stars.

As the sun rose, Judith found a new purpose. She shattered the window to Penny's room, twisted her way inside. With no other choice, Henry scooped Penny into his arms and put their life in the rearview mirror, racing toward an unknown future.

They stopped to rest in a nameless Texas town and met Jean, a just past middle-aged woman whose husband was murdered while securing provisions for their exodus. Henry, struggling to keep thoughts of war from his previous life at bay, was forced to take violent action to protect what remained of his family. The horde of Stargazers Henry had passed one hundred miles ago caught up to them, two of whom separated from the group to wander the motel parking lot keeping Henry, Penny, and Jean trapped inside for days.

Finally, Judith abandoned her patrol and attacked. Henry, Penny and Misfit, Jean's small dog, escaped as Jean distracted Judith.

Six months later, Henry and Penny are safe, but they haven't seen a sign of Jean.

Chapter One

You Deserved Better

Restraining Judith was like hugging a sack of cats. She clawed at Jean's flesh, gnashed her teeth, the enamel splintering. Ol' Reliable tossed a spray of gravel at the women as it careened out of the parking lot. For half a second, Jean caught sight of the eyes, somehow bright in the low morning light, of a girl she had only just met but already loved.

Pennies. Her eyes shone like pennies.

Jean smiled and relaxed her grip without realizing it. It was all the space Judith needed. She broke free, planted her bare foot on glass and gravel and took off as if the shards buried in her heels were springs.

"Shit!" Jean hissed, hugging the air Judith occupied a moment ago.

Judith's arms were pistons. If she felt the pain of her pulverized flesh, it was not apparent. She was halfway across the parking lot by the time Jean reached the motel room doorway. Judith would not catch up to Ol' Reliable. She would not fulfill her purpose, to eradicate her family. And she would not stop trying. Even as the glass and gravel punched deeper into the tissue, until it was flush with the surface of the skin. She would run trailing a river of blood until there was not enough for her heart to pump. On her knees, she would crawl, the river dwindling to a trickle until its headwaters expired.

Jean ran into the parking lot. In half a dozen steps, her lungs felt clogged like the neglected dryer lint trap when her husband, Marcus, was in charge of laundry. She took a painful breath and held it, muscles like spaghetti in a boiling pot. Judith would not stop. Maybe she was a passenger in her own body, seeing, hearing, and feeling everything. Maybe she understood her purpose and had no power to stop it. Maybe there was nothing left of her inside this walking shell.

POP

Judith shuddered but did not fall. A rosebud blossomed above her hip to the left of her spine.

"Hope y'all are far enough away you didn't hear that."

Another breath. The trigger was slick with sweat despite the chill in the air. Jean centered the crimson rose in the rifle's sights, then aimed above it and to the right a couple of inches. Her finger squeezed the trigger, not enough to fire.

The blood spread across Judith's back, a continent erupting from the baby blue sea of the jacket Henry forced her into the night he found her staring at the stars. Jean thought of her own husband, of turning the corner onto the soda aisle to discover him facedown, as if he had tripped while holding red paint cans. Killed in cold blood. Was this any better? Judith was a Stargazer, true, but that was not a choice.

The blossom swelled in size but shrank in the rifle's sight as she staggered away, movement slowed but no less determined. Jean found the trigger again, still warm to the touch.

POP

Judith took another step but found no earth beneath her. She crumpled as if her bones were made of sand.

"Goddammit," Jean whispered as Judith's arm lifted like a periscope. It plopped on the road, and she dragged herself forward half a foot at a time. The motherly instinct to protect Penny at any cost was corrupted inside of her, deconstructed by whatever force held her in place and forced her to watch the stars. Now, it propelled her forward by inches to make up an impossible distance. Not to protect. She writhed, leaving small, steaming puddles of herself on the asphalt.

Jean walked forward, an old memory unfurling.

"If you catch it, you kill it," her dad said.

That was fine. Jean never caught any fish worth keeping, until she did. The catfish bent her kid fishing pole into a rainbow but held on long enough for her dad to scoop it out of the water with his net. Her elation turned sour when he dumped the fish in the plastic bucket with two other keepers. Throughout the drive home she fretted about the fish, the echo of her dad's words louder than the George Strait cassette tape blaring through the truck's speakers. Each pothole reminded her of the THWOCK of the bat, the once living fish converted into a twitching thing, stunned, mouth gaping on autopilot.

The catfish squirmed on the cutting board, lips puckering as it searched the unfamiliar environment for oxygen. How long before the fish suffocated? Jean held a cleaver in one hand while the other hid her mouth.

"Come on, sugar. Just like cuttin' a watermelon!" her dad said, mussing her hair and helping himself to a beer.

Minutes passed, but how many more before the catfish stopped puckering like that? Wasn't it worse to die that way? Wouldn't a quick death be preferable?

That was a problem, though. Jean did not know if the death would be quick. What if she didn't cut all the way through, or missed and severed a fin instead?

"I can't do it, Daddy," she said with tears in her eyes. She didn't kill the fish, and the smell of it cooking sent her outside until the sun set.

"You deserved better," Jean said, hefting the rifle.

Judith's raspy breaths rattled like loose teeth inside her lungs. Fingers turned to claws gripped the asphalt, nails cracking and tearing. She no longer had the strength to pull herself.

If Jean could have spared the catfish's life, she would have. But for Judith, the only mercy was death. Her fingers relaxed and her body stilled, eyelids closing halfway so that only a sickle of brown showed. Jean sobbed and lowered the rifle. She knelt over the woman, Penny's mother. She grasped the corner of the item peeking from Judith's back pocket.

"Oh my. Oh my goodness," Jean said.

Penny smiled at her in picture form, a year younger, perhaps. She sat on the floor beside Henry, whose chest served as a table for her plastic tea set. He smiled as well, though his eyes stared ahead rather than at the camera. Penny held up a teacup as if offering it to the photographer, Judith, most likely.

She pressed the photograph to her chest and eyed the unwavering road. They were gone. Henry and Penny were gone. Misfit, too.

Would Henry turn around and come back for her?

Probably not, and for good reason. Either his wife was dead, or she was still intent on killing their daughter.

SKRICH

SKRICH

Jean's spine stiffened, joints popping as she turned her head to confront the noise. There had been two of them, two Stargazers who peeled away from the herd to patrol the motel parking lot. One was dead by her hand. The other ambled toward her, hobbling on a leg that could not support the weight of its body. The foot was a mangled clot of blood and cotton. It squelched under the slightest pressure, printing its strange shape on the asphalt.

What's your purpose? Judith wondered as she reclaimed the rifle from the road.

The Stargazer, a young man in a Texas Rangers shirt and flannel pajama bottoms, looked past her. His purpose was beyond the horizon.

SKRICH

SKRICH

His patchy beard accentuated the purple hollows of his cheeks rather than disguising them. He stepped around Judith's body, the ruin of his foot crunching wetly. He hesitated, injured leg spasming, and Jean swung the barrel toward him.

She swallowed, finding the trigger again.

His pajama bottoms snagged on a crack in the asphalt. He tripped but did not brace himself for the fall, his nose exploding like an overripe tomato falling off the cutting board. At once, he lifted his head showing shattered teeth like broken eggshells on his lips. His breaths formed bloody bubbles as he fought to stand, hem still snagged and foot as stable as a sponge.

"How many times am I going to have to do this?" Jean whispered.

Less than a week ago she had not heard the word *stargazer* used outside of its conventional meaning. In that world her biggest concern was nicotine withdrawal. Marcus was alive and excited by the thought of a summer road trip to see America's national parks.

POP

No more. And never again.

This was a new world, and Jean wasn't sure she belonged in it.

The road was a black river, straight save for the almost imperceptible curve pulling it west. There would be no road trip for her. Only chaos and suffering. Jean released the magazine and popped the top round free.

"Almost out," she mumbled.

If, she thought, it wasn't worth it to find Penny, Henry, and Misfit, she would only need one.

By midday, the clouds threatening rain hitched a ride on a quickening wind, revealing a sun that seemed incapable of warming the world beneath it. Jean left the bodies in the street. Though they deserved better, she did not have the strength to give it to them. She returned to the motel, shattered glass like diamonds spilled in a jewelry heist gone wrong. The power was out, and she had no fuel to refill the generator.

She sat on the bed in what had been Henry and Penny's room. The curtains billowed, growing pregnant with wind then collapsing only to balloon again moments later. The chill in the room, and the uneasy serenity of mayhem's aftermath played tricks with her mind. Had she dreamed it all? Conjured the kind man and his daughter to cope with her own loss?

Penny's books lay scattered across the comforter, suggesting she was reading to pass the time when Judith attacked. Jean knelt to the carpet and retrieved Misfit's leash, discarded during the turmoil of Judith's return. She wrapped the fabric around her fist and chewed the inside of her cheek.

"No, I didn't dream you," she said to the leash before tucking it into the pocket of her jeans.

As she pulled her hand free, she held the picture she'd stolen off Judith's corpse. They were not related. She barely knew them, but they were bigger in her memory than even Marcus.

Jean laughed at the thought of Penny barking into the phone, her way of saying good night to Misfit. She ran her thumb over the photograph and wondered what life would be like for that little girl. There would be no more tea parties, no mother to take her picture.

The rifle lay to her right, one path for her.

Ahead was an open door and the world beyond.

Jean returned the picture to her pocket. She would have to find a way to keep it safe until she saw them again.

In this part of Texas there were two things in abundance, guns and gas-guzzling vehicles. Jean confiscated the former when she encountered them but searched for an alternative to the latter. The neighborhood behind the grocery store across the street from the motel was a ghost town lacking only tumbleweeds. Front doors stood wide open. Detritus blanketed the sidewalks and lawns, as if vomited by the homes themselves. She found a Toyota Corolla idling in the middle of the street, a pool of oil spreading beneath it, operator nowhere in sight.

"Jesus," Jean whispered.

Scanning the driveways for a potential new ride, her eyes landed on the body of a woman. She lay on her side, clothes sodden with rain, death-stiffened limbs outstretched with hands forming two Cs, as if she had died strangling someone. Her left eye was a frozen vortex of gore. A Stargazer killed while attempting to fulfill its purpose? A domestic dispute taken to extremes on the precipice of the apocalypse?

Jean kept walking.

The wind rattled dead leaves in the trees, fastened to their branches by brittle stems. It was no longer *Texas cold* but just cold. The kind that made your fingers ache and your eyes water at the slightest gust. Jean's new jacket, pilfered from the foyer closet of a house still decorated for Christmas, was meant for a much larger woman. It swallowed Jean's thin frame but served a second purpose, hiding the two pistols she now wore against her ribs. Her backpack, taken from the same closet, was half-filled with protein bars and trail mix.

She breathed ghost clouds as she walked down the sidewalk. Lungs prickling, she cursed every cigarette she had smoked in her life while wishing she had one just then.

A dog barked, more as a question than a warning. Jean twirled as if spun by an invisible dance partner and scanned fence lines. Another bark followed by a solemn tattoo of a tail on wood. She jogged across the street, one arm keeping the pistols still against her body.

"Hello?"

The knocking sound increased in urgency.

"It's okay. It's okay," Jean said, pinpointing the fence and then unlatching it.

The dog wedged its dewy, black nose into the space created as Jean cracked the fence open.

"It's okay," she said again, then gasped when she saw the animal in full. "What are you, a polar bear?"

The dog's head was as big as an engine block, ears like white pizza slices. The backyard appeared invaded by spiders, webs of fur hanging like tinsel from tree branches, floating in the air like dandelion puffs. He had probably been trapped in the backyard for days, the sounds of civilization fading to wind in the trees.

"Hold on. It's okay," Jean said, hooking a finger under the collar and finding a bone-shaped identification tag. "Gunny."

His ears perked at the sound of his name, and he sank into a playful stance, front paws splayed and hind raised.

"Oh boy, you're gonna be a handful, huh?"

Demonstrating the truth of the prediction, Gunny head-butted the fence door the rest of the way open and barreled through it. In a breath he was gone, with the only evidence of his existence floating in the air like discarded tufts of cotton candy.

Stunned, Jean closed the gate. As she was considering whether freeing the dog was better than adopting him, she rounded the corner of the house to find Gunny waiting for her, hind raised and tail wagging.

"Oh, you are trouble, aren't you!" Jean said, only then remembering the leash in her pocket. It was intended for a dog hardly bigger than a house cat, but for the moment it would have to do. Gunny's demeanor changed the moment the leash clipped to his collar. He dragged Jean to the sidewalk and began to trot as if she was not a complete stranger, as if this walk was a daily routine between them. Together, they toured the neighborhood, Gunny marking mailboxes and fire hydrants, Jean testing car door handles. She found a small SUV with a nearly full tank of gas. The keys hung just inside the open door of the house.

"Wanna go for a ride?" she asked.

Gunny did. He hopped across the driver's seat and sat shotgun, head scraping the ceiling.

"You're like a white lion, aren't you? Look at all that fur!" Jean said, scratching the mane of longer hair encircling his neck.

She drove to the supermarket, Gunny pressing his nose to the window and grunting until she rolled it down for him. Jean could have searched for another supermarket. The Stargazers event happened so quickly few had time or the presence of mind to prepare. There would be other stores, pantries in abandoned houses. But she had a final task, one box to check before moving on.

Jean huffed, her fingers pooled in her lap like melted candle wax. She would never come back to this town, to this store. Whatever her destiny, it was beyond the horizon. Marcus' body was inside that building, the stain of his spilled blood on the tiles. Jean knew his body was not him, the man she loved. It was a vessel he used to navigate the world. But it was the vessel she loved, the vessel whose hands she held when she said *I do* for the third time but the first time she meant it.

"No free lunches, Gunny. You got a job now, understand? You protect me and I'll keep you fed."

Gunny followed her out of the SUV. The doors did not open automatically as she approached but offered minimal resistance as she pried them open. The power was out here as well. Jean sniffed. By the smell in the air, it had been out long enough for the milk to turn. Gunny sneezed, his much more sensitive nose reporting the same information.

"Alright, bud, let's find the most expensive shit they have. This one's on me," she said, wrangling a shopping cart free.

Gunny's claws, bred for gripping soil on steep mountainsides, screeched and squeaked over the tiles. Jean stopped before the toy section. A ghost of a chuckle passed through her lips as she recalled Henry showing her a doll in his shopping cart as proof he was just a dad out on an errand, that he wasn't a threat. Jean helped herself to a card game and coloring book.

Pet food was on the next aisle over. Jean hoisted a forty-pound bag into the cart and dumped cans of the most expensive wet food she could find on top of it. She eyed the sign hanging above the aisle to her left.

Water Soda Sports Drinks

She turned the corner and stopped. Marcus' bloodstain was like a black hole in the middle of the aisle. She smelled it, above the reek of spoiled milk, somewhere between burning wires and freshly turned soil. She tried to swallow and choked in the effort, tickling her lungs with saliva.

"Goddammit," she wheezed, eyes watering. "Not the way I wanted to say goodbye to you."

Gunny whined and backed away, pulling Jean with him.

"Hold on, boy. Just a second," she said, wrapping the leash around her knuckles.

Jean walked no closer to the site of her husband's death. She had memorized this exact scene without trying.

"Marcus, I'm leavin'. I came close to joinin' you. Awful close to it. Ain't a lot worth livin' for from what I can see of this world," Jean said, then dabbed her eyes. "Ain't a lot, but not nothin'. If I get to the point where there's nothin'... well, I'll cross that bridge when I get to it. Found this furry fella, and he's gonna keep me safe until I find Penny and Henry. Misfit, too. I don't guess she's gonna care for him much, but he'll have earned his place by then."

As if aware he was the topic of the conversation, Gunny rested his head against Jean's thigh and accepted her pets and scratches with almost cat-like purrs.

"Our story was only a few chapters in. But it was my favorite story. All those blank pages. We had so much more to do. So much more to see. I guess I'll see what I can and then tell you about it when I get to where you are. I love you, Marcus. Dyin' doesn't change that. Just means it's gotta be one-sided for a while."

Jean dragged Judith's body to a field beyond the motel parking lot, then did the same with her companion. The stiffness of their muscles beneath her fingers stirred the bile in her belly. Judith's arm felt like a bundle of rigid garden snakes. She draped them in blankets and anchored those in place with rocks. Easy work for a hungry scavenger, but with millions of dead bodies to choose from, maybe the inconvenience of the blankets would be enough.

"Said it before, but I mean it no less. You deserved better."

In the SUV, Jean adjusted the rearview mirror so that the motel was no longer visible. It was early in the afternoon by then, the sun beginning its decent to the west. She lowered the visor then turned on the radio, forgetting, for a moment, about the end of the world. Static mixed with emergency tones and silence. Toward the end of the dial, she found a station playing Spanish music, probably picked up from the other side of the border. The singer's voice was powerful, pained. Though she understood none of his words, Jean bit her lip to keep from crying. He was dead, most likely, as were the musicians, their talented fingers fat with bloat.

Two hundred thousand years of progress and one of the final testaments to mankind's soul was a dead man bellowing ranchera ballads from across the desolate Mexican desert.

Jean lowered the volume, stripping the urgency from the singer's voice, and pressed the gas. Gunny's interest in the outside world dissolved within a minute. He tilted to his left, eventually collapsing over the center console to rest his head in Jean's lap. His belly bulged with expensive kibble and a can of wet food more aromatic than the Dinty Moore meals Marcus favored.

"I'll join ya in a bit, Gunny. Just gotta put some miles under these tires."

She hoped she would find Ol' Reliable parked in front of a motel but didn't think Henry would take that option a second time. It was too close to the road, too exposed. His first motel stay nearly killed him twice over. He wouldn't put Penny in that sort of danger again. Likely, he would find a house well off the highway and park Ol' Reliable in a garage or behind a barn. It would not be easy to find them, but one thing Jean had in abundance was time.

An hour down the road the gas gauge showed its first noticeable movement, ticking to the left a hair. There were fewer trees and steeper hills, mesas like furry anvils in the distance. Cattle glared at her from behind barbed wire. Had they noticed the change in the world?

How many animals cowered behind fences, in zoos separated from a non-existent public by an insurmountable distance? Jean swallowed, clammy sweat speckling her brow, as she considered the plight of the dolphins in that theme park back in the city. One day the crowds, their trainers, just weren't there. Did they know the ocean was more than one hundred miles away? Could they sense the distance?

Gunny woofed softly in the midst of a dream. She couldn't help the dolphins, but at least she freed a polar bear.

This part of Texas felt as if it had already been abandoned, its apocalypse having left no witnesses. Sun-bleached barns like giant tortoises that died in a fruitless search for water dotted the landscape. Nature invaded the architecture, ripped it apart, a split board here, nail rusted to dust there. This was a land in stasis, a land waiting for the continents to shift and offer a new possibility. One of those in-between places on the map, a distance to cross to get to something better. Jean's attention was to the left and right, not ahead, and the danger much closer to her.

"Jesus Christ!" Jean screamed, slamming the brake pedal to the floorboard and wrangling the SUV onto the shoulder.

Gunny roared awake, barking at the roof as he writhed to right himself.

As she crested a hill, she met an ocean. The brakes locked and the tires skidded like a rock skipping across a pond. The SUV's bumper buckled a Stargazer's knee and he collapsed, disappearing beyond the hood.

"Oh my God!"

Jean's chin hovered over the steering wheel, the herd moving away from her like a tide in slow motion. Gunny showed his teeth, a growl so low in his throat it was barely audible. The man appeared in the rearview mirror, swaying for a moment, clothes striped with dirt from the tires. He walked forward, a drop of water returning to the sea.

In the past week, Jean had passed dozens of dead Stargazers, each facing the direction the herd was heading. They walked until their final breaths and died on the asphalt, arms outstretched to bring them inches closer to their final goal. They were so common Jean no longer saw them, like the mile markers and oil derricks that melted into the background of the world around her, there but too insignificant to notice, to pull a mind out of its daydreams.

"It's okay, big guy," Jean said, giving Gunny's mane a thorough scratch. He licked his lips, accepted the affection, then flashed his teeth at the mass drifting away from them.

Jean eased off the brake and the SUV crawled forward, because Henry and Penny were out there. The Stargazers were about fifteen bodies across, leaving, she hoped, enough room for her to skirt around the edge. As they approached the herd, Gunny began to growl again, flecks of spittle pebbling the window glass.

"You're okay, buddy."

She navigated the SUV to the culvert straddling the road, gently pressing the gas.

"Ugh," Jean said, the smell of blood and unwashed bodies filling the cabin. It was a sick smell, like garbage water and burning plastic. She shut off the heat and tugged her shirt over her nose, realizing at least some of the sour odor was her own. She sat taller in her seat but could not see the end of the herd, only the few hundred bodies immediately in front of her. They walked dreamlike, arms slack and eyes unfocused.

A man just beyond her door appeared to have been mauled, the fingers of his right hand like wet ribbons. Flies clotted around the meat, black bodies shiny with blood, little of which flowed then. Unless his purpose was to die belly-down, mouth full of asphalt and broken teeth, he would not fulfill it.

Shadows an unnamed shade between purple and gray stretched from the twisting fingers of mesquite. Jean flipped on the headlights, washing out the color of the Stargazers' sleep attire. She gave the engine a little more gas, challenging the SUV to live up to its name. A thought occurred, a snapshot elbowing aside the reality outside the window. She imagined the Stargazers turning their heads in unison, thousands of unfocused eyes finding a new purpose.

Jean shuddered as if a spider dipped beneath her collar to explore the ridges of her spine.

Then she saw it, a quick wink of fire within the crowd. Close enough to jab with a broom. A cigarette cherry. She knew it at once.

A smoking Stargazer? Jean lifted her foot off the gas pedal, allowing gravity to pull the SUV forward at a walking pace. She craned her neck, searching the haggard faces for the smoker.

"Can't see shit," she whispered.

Maybe it was the sunlight reflecting off a metal roof miles away. That made more sense than a Stargazer smoking. As this thought planted roots in her mind, she saw it again, and caught a fleeting glimpse of his face, his shifting eyes. He was not dressed like the others. He wore a visor hat, red most likely but the color was difficult to distinguish, and an apron, possibly green. His gait was different as well, not the hypnotized shuffle of the others but something more deliberate. He looked at the ground, matching his steps with the Stargazer in front of him so as not to entangle their feet.

"Is he ..."

Different and familiar. She did not recognize the young man, but felt she knew something about him. Jean could just keep driving, put the young man and his plight in her rearview mirror as she had done throughout her life. It felt better to leave, to move on and build a wall between her present and the hidden memories turning to fossils. There were many versions of Jean who would have done just that.

But not this one.

She pressed the horn. If the Stargazers intended to kill her, they would have done it. If what she suspected about the young man was true, this was how she would know. He flinched. The cigarette tumbled from his lips. Then he turned and looked at her.

Posted by Coloradokid_14 3 days ago

A Proposition for Those Who Remain

I did the math. It's rough, a guess at best. Using the number of people posting in this forum now vs one month ago, taking into account there may be people who are unable to post due to the circumstances of their surroundings, as well as the fact some people are posting who had not used the forum previously, I extrapolated this data as a model for the United States. Did I mention the math was rough? It's very rough.

About 80,000. That's how many of us are left. You can pad that with 20K on either side. If 100,000 is sexier to you, go ahead and run with that.

A college football stadium with room in the nosebleeds. I haven't seen a non-Stargazer in over a week, though I am not going out of my way to find them.

I've seen the other posts. I know what's happening out there.

Look, we don't know what this is. We can guess. There are some brilliant thoughts in this very forum. Still, I don't think we will understand the why or how in the same way an ant won't understand why or how its hill was turned into a tortilla by a bumbling toddler. It won't recognize the connection between the tread marks and the devastation.

Our hill is gone, and our families are dead or as good as dead. And I'm getting off track.

They did it. Whoever *they* are. And we remain, for now. What is to become of us? How do we survive?

Communication.

Communities in a looser sense of the word.

I don't suggest we attempt to recreate our fallen cities. The larger the number of us gathered, the more of us that can be killed in one action. We need communication of threats, of opportunities. We need a loosely linked community to mitigate our personal shortcomings. I, for example, have never grown a tomato plant capable of bearing fruit. We need to think beyond the expiration dates of canned goods.

How do we do this? How do we share information across millions of square miles?

Safely.

This forum will go away. The infra-structure is crumbling. Whether by a deliberate act or simple neglect, we will not be able to communicate sooner than later. Here's my idea. Mailboxes and ham radios.

Still with me?

Good.

I don't imagine mailboxes are going to be a high priority for demolition. They might not be accounted for at all. I've included a map of around sixty mailboxes between the U.S. and Canada. (Apologies to Mexico, wanted to get this out there before I ran out of time.) These are all off interstates or state highways. How do we use mailboxes? I view them as message boards for our time, like how we have used this forum over the past two weeks. Helping each other. Tips, tricks, and intel. Have something to share? Know where to find clean water? Drop a note and raise the mailbox flag.

Radios. A lot to learn, I suggest you find an electronics store before they're turned to dust. Grab a ham radio and spare batteries. If this is going to work, I'll need some help with repeaters to spread the message further. After I post this, I'm hopping over to Google. Hopefully, I'll be back with more to share.

Chapter Two

You're Gonna Have to Make a Choice

There was no comfortable path forward. No easy life regardless of the decision she made at that moment. Life would only be varying degrees of terrible, peppered with moments of happiness that would only ever be an imitation of another world's beauty. No easy paths, but the two before her were not equal in their potential to complicate her immediate future. Jean left an agitated Gunny in the SUV and ran to catch up to the smoker.

"Hey!" she called.

He flinched, the rhythm of his shuffle thrown off. His widened eyes stared at the pelt of matted hair of the woman in front of him. Jean could drive away. She could aim the SUV at that terrible destination, which would be an easier path than this one.

"It's okay," she said, and the young man's spine stiffened. His eyes darted to the right. "What's your name?"

The stench crawled into her nostrils, blossomed in her throat and lungs. Sweat, piss, blood, and feces. A toxic perfume just to the left of putrescence. The Stargazers shuffled in a close group, their steps not synchronized but in some sort of order that prevented collisions. Jean matched his pace. What if the Stargazers faced her then? Gunny was trapped in the SUV, his bark no longer audible. All the weapons in the world wouldn't matter if the herd found a new purpose.

Jean walked a few additional paces, trying to get the timing right.

"1, 2, 3!" she said, then inserted herself between two Stargazers. The action caused a ripple effect, Stargazers tripping and falling, knocking neighbors to the ground. None extended a hand to break their fall. Self-preservation must have been left out of their marching orders. More fell. A dozen, then many dozens. Most, but not all, regained their footing. Some did not rise, their periscope heads kicked by the herd still moving forward.

Kicked and kicked.

Stepped on and smashed.

Flattened, but Jean couldn't think about it.

"Michael? That's your name?" she said.

She could barely read his name tag in the late afternoon light.

He swallowed, concentrated harder on the Stargazer in front of him. There was a war behind his eyes, twin canals of peach flesh below them, the paths of his tears through grime.

"Have you been walking this whole time, Michael?"

He swallowed again. She almost asked him *why,* then she caught a glimpse of the woman beside him. The same brown hair and defined cheekbones. His nose was a replica of hers, though slightly larger. Her attire indicated her transition occurred before sleep. She wore a polo shirt with a fast-food burger logo over the left breast, jeans, and non-slip shoes that were beginning to come apart.

"Oh no," Jean whispered, noticing his finger curled inside her belt loop. "Michael, is … is that your mother?"

Their eyes met for the first time, his two trembling sacs of jelly threatening to either burst or collapse. His lips were chapped raw, ears cherry red from the cold. How had he survived this long? Maybe he and his mother had not come from San Antonio, seventy or eighty miles to the east. Maybe they were from one of the small towns along the way. No food. No water except what fell from the sky.

"Hey, it's okay, Michael. I'm here to help. I-I'm trying to catch up with some friends. We were … separated. We're gonna look for a place, a safe place to ride this thing out. Or at least figure out what's next."

Hope and fear flickered across his face. Michael kept walking, head turning toward the woman beside him.

"Michael? You're gonna have to make a choice. It's an awful choice, but it'll be the most important decision of your life. You can come with me. I've got a vehicle a little way back. I'll get you warm and fed," Michael licked his lips. "Or you can stay with your mama. I know that's what you *want* to do. I wanted to stay with my husband, but the Universe had other plans. If you follow your mama, it's only gonna take you one place. The end. If you go with me, well, maybe it'll be different. Better."

Michael glanced at her and then at his black, non-stick shoes, which squelched with each step. Sweat or blood, Jean hoped for the former.

"We can get more cigarettes…"

Michael mumbled, more an expression of pain than a semblance of thought.

This isn't working, Jean thought, shuddering as her fingers grazed the thigh of the Stargazer in front of her. She could taste them, polluted breaths and unwashed bodies. The film on her tongue tasted like spoiled mayonnaise and sea water.

And the sun was almost down, shadows thinning as the darkness deepened. Dusk approached, and she was surrounded by Stargazers.

"Michael? Do you like dogs?"

***

"It's okay, Gunny! It's okay!" Jean said, returning to the still running SUV with Michael trailing behind. The dog spun in circles on the front seat, giving life to a whirlwind of white fur.

"He's big!" Michael said, his voice a couple octaves higher than she might have guessed. Though he was not an imposing man, only an inch or two taller than Jean and just as lanky, his tone was pre-pubescent.

"He is! That's Gunny. I found him in a backyard earlier today. He's gonna be my protector."

Michael tapped on the window, "Hi Gunny! I'm Michael!"

Inside the SUV, Gunny crawled over the seat as if scaling a mountain. He pinned Michael and let his nose explore the new scents. The young man laughed, held his hands up in mock surrender as Gunny's tongue found tasty strips of exposed skin.

"Just give him a little nudge, Michael," Jean said, then wondered if he would have the strength to do it. Michael might have been walking for days, she remembered. How many days had it been, now? That he would have found time to eat was unlikely. "Treat, Gunny? Treat!"

Gunny bounded over the center console and sat expectantly, a paw hovering.

"I'm glad you knew that one, boy. You're like ten puppies in a dog costume!"

Gunny planted his paw on Jean's thigh, eyes locked onto hers as if anticipating betrayal.

"Michael, can you grab a biscuit out of the bag at your feet? There's plenty to eat in the bags on the other side. Water, too. Have as much as you need."

Michael rummaged through three bags before finding the biscuits.

"You can give it to him," Jean said, and he did.

A few seconds later, she felt a tap on her shoulder, "Can you open it for me?"

Jean took the bottle of water, twisted the cap off, and passed it back. To her right, Gunny crunched the biscuit into morsels. From behind, Michael chugged the water, breathing through his nose so we would not have to remove the bottle from his lips.

"This one too," he said, tapping her shoulder again.

Five bottles later, Jean put the SUV into drive and crawled forward. To the west, the sun was no longer visible, its light flaring in a dozen colors as if in mockery of the darkness trailing. The Stargazers, those not captured by the headlights, were silhouettes then. That was easier to stomach, black shapes instead of something still resembling human. Michael peppered Jean with questions, mostly about Gunny, but fell silent and shifted in his seat as Jean pressed the gas.

"Everything okay?" Jean asked, adjusting the rearview but only capturing a sliver of his turned head.

"Mama ..." he said, breath fogging the glass.

Jean slowed the SUV.

"You want to tell her goodbye? Tell her you love her?"

She lowered the window for him.

"I love you, Mama! I love you!" he said, voice wavering as if a struck tuning fork had been pressed against his throat. "I love..."

Michael didn't finish the sentence. Instead, he raised the window and reclined in his seat, silent save for a hitch in his breath.

"That love doesn't end, Michael. Leavin' your mama behind doesn't change a thing about it. You're gonna carry that with you forever. She's gonna be a passenger in your heart forever," Jean said, drawing a steadying sigh from him. "She would have wanted you to go. I don't know your mama, but I know that's what she would have wanted. No parent wants their child to suffer. I never had kids, but I've been a parent before, plenty of times. Sometimes doin' the right thing can feel like the worst thing, because the love is so big you can't see past it. You're just gonna have to trust me for a little while. There's somethin' better for you past it."

A few more seconds passed in silence, the sound of Michael's breathing settling. The herd went on, splitting like water around a boulder where a Stargazer fell. Jean could not see the end of it even with the brights on. Out of the corner of her eye, Jean saw Michael's bony fingers emerge from the backseat. He burrowed them into Gunny's fur.

Jean turned the radio on. The Spanish station hung on, sizzling with static. It was better than nothing. There was much to say, but any words she might share felt too small for the moment, too insignificant.

Half an hour passed before she reached the head of the herd and was able to return to asphalt. Gunny snored beside her, Michael's hand still within the forest of his fur. She glanced behind to find his head resting against the passenger seat. His lips, red as a cigarette cherry, were parted with slaver dangling like spider silk.

Apocalypse Radio

Call me CK. For those of you who followed my posts, you might know me as Coloradokid_14. I wonder if Coloradokids underscore 1-13 made it. Probably not, but if you did let me know.

I don't imagine there's a lot of you listening yet. But I have heard from folks on both coasts and some in the middle thanks to the repeaters. They're helping me spread the word. At the end of this broadcast, I'll share the locations of the mailboxes again.

So, how do we utilize this platform? I imagine the hundredth iteration won't resemble the first. What I mean to say is ... well, you remember podcasts? Remember finding a podcast you loved and going back to the first episodes? Sometimes felt like a whole different program. It takes a while for something like that to find its legs, to figure out what it wants to be. For Apocalypse Radio, I just hope we make it to one hundred episodes.

Let's start with now. The world as we know it is gone. Most of our friends and relatives are dead or in a hurry to get there. If you have a family member with you, consider yourself lucky. Lucky in the grand scheme. I heard from two brothers in New

Mexico that made it, a couple of friends from Massachusetts hiding out in Maine. Why the world is gone...well, that's what we're all waiting to find out, isn't it?

The conspiracy boards lit up during the first few days, but this didn't fit any narrative. Doesn't seem to be the government. Did you see the picture of that Senator walking with the 'Gazers? As far as I can tell, there was nothing unusual happening at Groom Lake, the Denver Airport, or Mount Weather. If I recall, the Georgia Guidestones suggested five-hundred million as the global population target. If this had anything to do with those that was a gross overestimation.

Where the conspiracists ran out of ideas, the religious nuts stepped in. They had lots of answers, and most could hold water as well as a wicker basket. It's not quite The Rapture, but it certainly feels biblical. I'm not a religious person. If you are and this was foretold in one of your texts, please let me know. I've got a bone to pick with whoever you call God.

There's another theory. To be honest, it scares me most of all. I can cope with manmade bullshit. I could understand if this was some lab experiment that got out of control. I ain't sold on it being from God yet, so that leaves us with another prevalent guess. You know the one. Remember that post about the failed Stargazer? Could have been a troll, but if not ... Jesus, I can't think of anything more terrifying.

I'd rather not speak about it. I'm afraid I'll will it into existence if it isn't already fact. But I don't think it was a coincidence they were looking at the night sky.

(Sighs)

I do have some mail to share. It isn't good, so if you're looking for tips and tricks to survive the apocalypse, that might have to wait until next time. This was found in a mailbox off I-40 in Arizona. It was radioed in yesterday. I tried to record it, but the audio's not the greatest. So, I'll just read what I transcribed.

"I don't know if this is the right mailbox. I followed the directions, and this seems to be the closest one. Without a cell this shit's a lot tougher to figure out.

I made it out of L.A. What a fucking nightmare. I know it's bad out there for everyone. There are just so many of us there...or were, I guess. It wasn't my intent to follow the Stargazers on my way out of the city. We were just using the same road. But I did catch up to them. I thought a bike was a better choice than a car, and I was glad for it then. No way I could have made it around them. I was on I-10, I think, near Joshua Tree. The Stargazers turned off the road. I should have kept going, but I didn't. I was curious. I turned with them, the smooth asphalt transitioning to rough earth. The river of people became a blur on the horizon.

There was smoke the direction they headed, but that's not strange for California. Seems like wildfire season is all year, now.

I wish it was wildfires. God, do I wish it.

It was a pit. A pit the Stargazers had apparently dug. It was also on fire, and it was full of Stargazers. They walked into the pit, caught fire, and kept walking until their bodies failed them. There were Stargazers around the pit, some with poles and some with shovels. The ones with poles kept the fire going, helped spread it to those not fully engulfed. Sometimes the Stargazers fell, and the fire went out. Then they just waited there, waited to catch fire again. Those with shovels buried the remains.

My mom might have been among them. My dad and siblings, friends and former lovers. Them and everyone else congealing in the flames, skin melting together. A human soup bubbling at the bottom of the pit like a pot you accidentally let simmer overnight.

A Stargazer's pole bent, the metal weakening due to the fire. She examined it for a moment, tested its functionality. It bent further. She dropped it and jumped onto the pile of smoldering bodies. She caught fire after a few paces and kept walking, just like the others. Her feet sank into the muck, the boiling fat and brittle bones. She was stuck, like quicksand in the old cartoons. She tried to move toward the larger flames, but every shift of her body made her sink a little more.

I turned away. I could do nothing for them.

I share this message as a warning. If you see smoke, and especially if you come across a group of Stargazers headed toward it ... turn away."

Jesus ... (sighs)

I shared that for a reason. Yes, it's awful. Yes, it's repulsive. It's also important. The Stargazers are reaching the end of their usefulness. Of their utility. I imagine we will see more of this in the coming days and weeks. What comes next? When there are no Stargazers? When it is just those of us who were not turned?

Maybe the answer will come from the skies. Maybe we'll be culled in round two.

On a different note, there were reports during the first few days, reports of well-meaning folks freeing zoo animals en masse. Apparently, that was more widespread than I initially believed. Imagine what this continent will look like in twenty or thirty years. Multiple generations of lions, tigers, and … well, the bears were already here. Elephants and rhinos. Many won't survive, but some will.

Life always finds a way.

CHAPTER THREE

WE'LL GO ON

There were no signs of humanity beyond the herd, only evidence of its recent peril. Abandoned cars and trucks, including one parked neatly on the shoulder, its windows raised and painted crimson from the inside. Jean ensured Michael was asleep before slowing the SUV for a better look. She detected no movement within the sedan, and the blood looked dark, reflecting no light. The four-person stick figure family above its bumper wore Mickey Mouse ears, as did the caricature of a dog.

Probably for the best.

She thought this and then cursed herself for thinking it. No, there had to be a reason to keep going. Even if it wasn't obvious to her then. Even if it was only to serve as a buffer between vulnerable people and the misery stalking them like a shadow.

The gas tank ticked toward one-third full, and the distance between stations was growing. She would need to find a place to rest for the night or risk being stranded on the road. Armed, and with a wolf-sized dog that would at least put up a good front, it was still not a place she wanted to be. Since pulling into the parking lot of the grocery store with Marcus, Jean had encountered five non-Stargazer people. Forty percent of them committed murder or attempted to.

Jean leaned forward, squinting at the sign at the far end of her headlights.

"I gotta pee!" Michael screamed.

Jean briefly lost control of the SUV, and it rumbled off the road. Gunny woke with rage in his throat, teeth gleaming at his reflection in the window.

"Jesus Christ, Michael!" Jean said.

As she placed a hand to her chest, a pinkie resting on the butt of the firearm she'd secured there. Gunny growled at the window, seeking a point of focus for his rage.

"I gotta pee now!" Michael yelled, clawing at the door handle.

"Okay, okay! Let me pull over first!" Jean said, pressing the brake and easing onto the shoulder.

The door was open before the SUV fully stopped. Michael tumbled out and rolled over gravel losing his apron in the process. He waddled forward, jeans sliding to his knees. In between the scraping sound of his shoes over dirt there was a whisper of liquid pummeling dry earth.

"Ahhh ... oh, shoot!" Michael said, leaning to the side as the stream dwindled and crept toward his jeans.

"Suppose we should follow suit," Jean told Gunny, and clipped the leash to his collar. "I'm gonna make water over here, Michael. Give me some privacy please."

"Okay!" Michael shouted, his body like a bow, the urine then just a trickle.

Gunny waited for Jean to finish and then added to her puddle, his obsidian eyes narrowing at the darkness.

"Hear somethin' Gunny boy?"

It was more likely a smell than a sight. Beyond the wash of the SUV's headlights, Jean could only guess the structure of the landscape. There were stars overhead, a moon wrapped in Earth's shadow, and nothing else. No house or streetlights. Not even a lightning bug this far west.

"Better?" Jean said, smiling.

Michael nodded, "Can we wait a few minutes? I think I might have to go again."

"Of course. How 'bout we let Gunny stretch his legs? He was cooped up in that yard for at least a few days."

She offered Michael the leash. He finished tying his apron and reached for it as if it might be a snake in disguise.

"Go ahead," Jean said. "Did you have a dog, Michael?"

He gave the leash a little tug and smiled when Gunny responded by turning around and following his lead.

"Um, yeah. When I was younger. When my daddy left, Mama found out she couldn't do it on her own. She couldn't take care of me and a dog. We had two. They were little ones, the hot dog kind?"

"Dachshunds?"

"Yeah, that's right," Michael said, then smiled. "I used to get extra sweaty so they would lick it off. Mama thought it was gross. She hated the sound of it. Sometimes when I was supposed to take a shower I just stood there with the water on.

The doggies didn't like the soap. I'd get a bit wet in case Mama checked my towel, but I wouldn't use soap. Mama could always tell, though."

Gunny trotted to the shoulder, found a suspicious tuft of grass, and marked it.

"It sure is different without all the lights, huh?" Jean said.

Michael shook his head, posture stiffening.

"What? What's wrong, Michael?"

"Not s'posed to look up. That's what happened to Mama. She looked up and ..." he trailed off, shaking his head again.

Jean nodded and gently grasped his elbow, "I guess no one knows, do they? No one knows what happened. The way I see it, the difference is you havin' control over wanting to look at the stars. I don't think your Mama, or anyone she was walkin' with, looked up at the stars because they wanted to. They were made to do it. For whatever reason, we weren't."

Michael nodded, "I'm afraid to."

Jean squeezed his elbow, "I get it. I've been more afraid these last few days than anytime my whole life. You can look up in your own time. But, Michael, I've never seen the sky like this. Not since I was a little girl, anyway. My folks used to take us campin' and my dad was always set on not payin' for it. He'd take us into the forest, not the woods. The woods were where we used to play and build forts. He took us into the *forest* so far from people if a single thing went wrong there'd be no rescue for us."

Jean gently turned him around, leading him back toward the SUV. Gunny alternated sniffing the road and glaring at things he could not see.

"Usually, it was too thick to see much. Just little glimpses of sky above the treetops. Sometimes, though, he'd lead us to a meadow and lookin' up felt like bein' at the bottom of the sea. It looks that way now. You can see every star, the Milky Way. Ever seen the Milky Way, Michael?"

He scratched behind his ear, "I've eaten a few. They're not my favorite, but I'd never say no to a candy bar."

Jean rolled her lips inside her mouth to keep from laughing. She did not know how sensitive Michael might be to laughter.

"They're not my favorite either. I'm partial to Twix. But I'm talkin' about something different than candy. The galaxy. Do you know what a galaxy is?"

Michael rolled his head rather than shaking or nodding. Jean interpreted this to mean he had heard the term but likely could not offer a definition.

"The solar system is our star, the sun, and all the planets that go around it. Got it? Earth, Jupiter, Saturn. The Milky Way is a galaxy, and it has billions of stars, billions of suns. You ever see a hurricane on TV?"

Michael nodded.

"The galaxy is like that but with stars. Instead of clouds it's stars and other planets. Now, I've about reached the limit of my astronomy trivia, but I do know it used to be easy to see, the galaxy," Jean said, then stopped and perched her hands on her hips. "You kinda forget it's even there. Kinda forget how small we are, just hangin' out by our average little star."

Michael shielded his eyes as if stepping out of a dark room into full sun. He peeked through splayed fingers.

"Over there," Jean said, nudging his chin.

The gaps between his fingers widened, and then his hand fell to his side.

"Wow, it's ..." he began.

"It's beautiful. I'd trade havin' my old life back in a heartbeat, but it is beautiful."

"Jean?"

"Yes?"

Michael held out Gunny's leash, "I have to pee again."

Jean followed the signs to an RV park. She drove around it three times with the window rolled down, listening for signs of life. Several spots were vacant, and the chaos of overturned lawn chairs and tipped ice chests suggested an exodus undertaken in haste. She saw no lights in the windows, but she thought there was electricity, for now. Through parted blinds, she saw the green glow of a microwave's clock. As well, one large streetlight at the far end of the lot still functioned, its sodium-orange radiance stirring memories of October. The air wavered between chilly and frigid, the latter usurping the former. Had it smelled of campfires or cider, Jean might have thought her months were off.

Had it only been days? A week, maybe? When had she first heard the term, Stargazer? It must have been on the news. It happened so quickly, the reality shifting so completely it was like someone had applied a tourniquet between her life before and her life after. Only a trickle of memories seeped through, more impressions than concrete thoughts. Echoes shouted through the veil.

"Jean?" Michael mumbled, as if sinking into a dream.

"Yes?"

"I have to pee again."

She placed the SUV in park. Jean was not confident in the decision, but exhaustion overpowered her caution. The door to the RV nearest to her was open, flapping slightly in the breeze.

"Good timing. We're stoppin' for the night. I'm gonna grab Gunny and take a peek inside before I commit to it. Follow me but stay outside until I come fetch you."

Gunny sampled the air. A low growl was his apparent default setting when encountering new scents. His tail wagged in lazy half-circles, head tilting as he searched for sounds to scrutinize.

"Come on Gunny boy," Jean said, giving the leash a twitch.

Michael followed as directed. He folded his arms over his chest, the crisp desert breeze coaxing the hair to stand erect. Jean withdrew the weapon from the inner pocket of her coat. Michael's eyes swelled, and he retreated a step as he recognized Jean's firearm for what it was.

"Oh, I don't like 'em either," Jean said, taking notice. "But not liking 'em and not using 'em are two different things. Might have to show you how soon."

She climbed into the RV and waited, listening. There was an electric hum of what she hoped was a refrigerator. The tinkling of blinds against window glass.

"Hello?" she said.

Gunny whined and shifted in the gravel. Jean showed him the palm of one hand and arched her eyebrows the way she had when silently chastising Marcus.

Jean took a step up and then stopped. There was a new sound, or at least one she had not recognized. Something like sizzling. Burning wire? She swallowed the lump floating in her throat.

"Hello?" she said, a bit louder.

From over her shoulder, she heard Michael moan in relief and the sizzling subsided.

"Jesus, Michael."

***

She thought sleep would be difficult to come by. It often was for her in unfamiliar places. But, after a dozen trips between the SUV and their new living space, Jean's eyes felt like two dry balloons about to pop. She locked the door, told Gunny to lay beside it, which he immediately disobeyed, and collapsed on a small couch with fabric as rough as a two-day beard. Michael fell asleep in what served as the main bedroom without taking his shoes off.

The RV was as cold as a walk-in cooler as Jean blinked the sleep out of her eyes. Her breath billowed in a puff of steam. The chill upon waking had a snap to it. Not sharp enough to penetrate her jacket, but enough to fill her cheeks with needles.

"Cold front musta come through," she said to Gunny, whose cinderblock of a head pressed into her navel.

Michael snored in his bed. She was careful not to wake him as she retrieved her gun, wrangled Gunny, and escorted him outside. Michael needed rest, and Jean did not know how frequent his opportunities to have it would be.

The time of day was impossible to guess. Sometime between dawn and lunch, she imagined, but the sun hid behind a haze of fog making it hard to tell. Gunny tugged her toward clusters of foliage, frozen in time since last summer, and doused them in steaming piss.

"That doesn't hurt you to just cut the stream off like that? Marcus used to get so mad if I interrupted him while he was peein'. Said that pee would find another way out of his body."

Beyond the sound of Gunny's snorts, the whisper of his urine over unsuspecting leaves, there was no sound. No drone from the highway, no birds singing their hopes for a springtime tryst.

It was an underwater stillness, a stasis. One only possible at the end of the world.

Back inside, Jean attempted to conform her morning routine to their new surroundings. Everything was a scaled down version of what she was accustomed to. The toilet felt like a plastic toy, one that might crack under her insubstantial weight. The stove could barely accommodate a pot and a pan at the same time. And always there was a pony-sized canine pasting himself to a thigh.

She whipped up a passable breakfast of grits, eggs, and toast. Seconds before she would have called Michael to eat, he emerged, still dressed for work, eyes blinking and two hands hovering over his crotch.

"It's right there," Jean said, nodding to the bathroom. "But don't get accustomed to it. Probably gonna have to start goin' outside if we plan on stayin' here."

She could have finished her breakfast in the time it took Michael to empty his bladder.

"Feel better?" she asked.

He nodded and licked his lips at the sight of the breakfast she prepared.

"For me?"

She smiled, "For us."

Michael ate as if it might be his last meal. She refreshed his plate with fried eggs twice before he finally reclined and rested his hands on the small hill of his belly.

"How did it happen with your mama?" Jean asked.

It was a conversation they needed to have, and Jean saw little value in delaying. She would share her story about Marcus, strafing the grittier aspects. And she would inform him of her task, to reunite with the only other good people she had met since the world ended.

Michael's eyes bulged as if he'd stepped on a nail, and he found a refrigerator magnet to fixate on as he processed the request.

"Don't mean to cause pain, Michael. I just need to understand what you've been through."

Michael nodded and sat up. He licked his lips and turned his attention back to the magnet.

"How about we chat about it for a bit? If it gets too tough, we'll move on. I'll get the shower runnin' and we can clean ourselves up and then head into whatever passes for a town out here. Need to stock up on cigarettes, right?"

Michael nodded, a smile threatening.

He sighed and turned his gaze to Jean for a moment, then settled on staring at his own hands as he spoke. His voice was lower, the words coming in twos and threes.

"She was at work. We work close together. Not the same place. We used to, but Mama didn't like it when the boss ladies talked to me stern. Got her in trouble before," he said, smiling at a memory. "I finish workin' before Mama. I walk over to her place. Sometimes I wait inside and eat. Usually, I wait outside and smoke or fall asleep in the car. Mama counts the money and she's always the last one."

He stopped, pink tongue resting on his bottom lip. His nostrils flared as tears welled. Jean reached across the small table and draped her hand over his.

"It's okay," she said.

Michael nodded and cleared his throat, "Mama works two jobs. She used to work three but can't do it no more. Couple times she was late comin' out it was 'cause she fell asleep in the back. It was past midnight, and I already smoked about five cigarettes. I been in and out the car 'cause it was cold outside. Mama was late and I was ready to go home. Thought she mighta fallen asleep again, so I headed to the back, and ..."

Jean squeezed his hand as Michael looked to the side.

"She was outside. She had a buncha lil' papers in one hand like she got up in the middle of doin' the money and decided to go for a walk. Smoke maybe? She don't smoke no more. Used to. She did once or twice since she quit, but it's been years. She was lookin' up at the sky. I looked, too, thinkin' maybe she saw a saucer or somethin' but it was just stars. I asked Mama what she was doin' and she didn't say anything. I tapped her shoulder, and she didn't say anything. It was like she was inside her own mind," Michael said, then locked eyes with Jean. "I know how that feels, to be stuck inside your own mind. Sometimes it's hard to make the words in my head come out the way I want 'em to."

Jean nodded, "Me too. Seems like I know fewer words now than when I was young."

Michael freed a hand and patted the pocket of his shirt where Jean guessed he kept his cigarettes. Not finding any, he continued.

"I shook her and got louder. Got scared and then mad. We heard stuff about other people goin' dumb. That's a mean word, and I don't like to use it, but ..." he trailed off, then tapped his head. "I guess I don't know the nice word."

"Stargazers. That's what they call 'em."

Michael nodded, licked his lips as if he was about to attempt to speak it, but then shook his head.

"I didn't know what to do. I was scared and mad. I tried to call Aunt Barbara, but she didn't answer. I called Mama's boss, too. I went back to the parking lot and yelled for help, but there wasn't no one around. None of the cars in the road stopped. I know a lot of bad stuff was goin' on and I just didn't wanna believe it was ... it was happenin' to Mama."

Michael picked up a fork and began to scrape dried yolk off the tines.

"I shook Mama, and it was like shakin' one of my dolls when I was a kid. Thought she might break her neck, so I stopped. I said bad things to her to try and make her come back. I thought if I said the awfullest thing I could think she would have to come back. But she didn't."

Michael folded his hands in his lap, air streaming out of his nostrils as sobs built pressure in his body.

"It's okay, Michael. Whatever happened is okay."

His next words came as a whisper, "I couldn't save her. Mama tried to keep the bad from me, but Jeff and Seamus from work told me about it. Said people was turnin' to zombies or something. Like those movies they play at Halloween. Said there was other bad stuff too, and then both of 'em didn't show up for work."

Michael swallowed, Adam's Apple rising and falling like the puck of a carnival strongman game. He placed his hands on the table and did not resist when Jean tented hers over them.

"I stayed with her all night. It got colder, so I brought her coat out but couldn't get her arms inside. So, I put it over her shoulders like that shawl she sometimes wore inside the house. Think I fell asleep, 'cause next thing I knew she was walkin' away and it was a bit light out. Her coat fell off and I scooped it up and put it back on. She kept walkin' and I kept followin' and then there was more of 'em. The star-people?"

"Stargazers."

"There was more of 'em. I just followed. Didn't know what else to do. I-I couldn't leave my mama. She wouldn'ta left me. We ... we walked for so long. It rained. It got cold at night. I th-thought I was gonna walk until I died."

Michael turned toward the door, where Gunny slept on his back, paws in the air.

"You think she made it to us? You think she's still out there?"

Jean exhaled a measured breath. Michael's hope was like a wayward kite. Her words, the wind. The wrong combination could send him into the atmosphere beyond her reach. They could also send him spiraling in the opposite direction.

"She might be, but not as you knew her. That's somethin' you're gonna have to accept. It'll be the worst thing you'll ever have to believe, but it's the one thing that'll keep you going. My Marcus is gone. I know it 'cause I saw his body. You don't have that. That's a good *and* bad thing. Good because you don't have the memory of it. Bad because you'll always have that doubt. Maybe she was the one, maybe the only one, who came around. But, Michael, just know if that did happen, she would come back to you."

"So I ..." Michael began.

"So, you go take a shower. I'll see if I can't find some new clothes for you. Then we take Gunny for a ride and help ourselves to some cigarettes. Don't ever stop thinkin' about her. But try ... try not to lose yourself looking for her. And we'll go on, Michael. We'll go on."

Apocalypse Radio

W hat was it Bob Dylan said about the weatherman and the wind? Well, you might need one to tell you there's a storm coming. So, this is me doing just that. Heard from some friends in the northwest there was a two-day storm that finally passed yesterday. What I can't do, for now at least, is forecast where the hell it's going. But don't these things usually go west to east? That's standard, isn't it?

Assuming at least that much hasn't changed about the world, some of you will be getting wet soon. Much of our options for shelter are gone. If you were waitin' for a sign to find a better roof, this is it.

I've got some news of a more speculative nature to share, but for those of you hearin' this, please spread the word. If this attempt at community ends up being a dozen sad men in bunkers, we might as well use what remains of our lives pranking the archaeologists of future civilizations. Here's an idea for when the end is near. Shove a bunch of Easter eggs, the plastic ones, up your ass and then walk into a bog. The bog will preserve the body, and the eggs will be discovered when the corpse is exhumed. Maybe hide something inside the eggs?

A joke, of course, but it raises the question of who that future archaeologist will be. What do you imagine? Will it be what or whoever caused this? Or will another species, currently on the planet, evolve to humanity's level of intellect? I'm betting on rats. Always love an underdog.

I think my anxiety is coming through, and for that I apologize. My ambition is not to turn this platform into a joke. I debated the Easter eggs bit and would probably take it back now if I could. As important as humor is in the face of horror, it's not what you need right now. You need information. You need insight into hidden dangers in the topography. I'm static for the moment, but many of you aren't. Many of you are fightin' for your lives. I have nothing to offer you beyond the weather, and something incomplete but potentially important.

I was contacted an hour or so ago. If you are listening, and you'll know it's **you** I'm referring to momentarily, please try again.

I didn't make a recording. That will change in the future. I'm making a trip into what's left of the nearest town to scrounge as many supplies as I can. I'll see if I can't improve my equipment in the process.

Anyway, back to the message. It was just a handful of words. *Gone. Monument. Ugly.*

That's it. I have a guess but will sit on it for now. As I said, if you are the person, a young woman by the sound of it, who contacted me please try again.

Wasn't there an old mystery about the Carolinas, some settlers who vanished and left behind a single word? I may be getting my history mixed up, but it feels familiar.

Spring is comin', folks. It isn't here yet, but it's comin'. While in town, I'm going to stock up on seeds. I suggest you do the same. What's left on the shelves won't be good forever. If you ask me, much of it wasn't good to begin with. I've eaten so much canned meat in the past week I think I might be preserving myself from the inside out. I guess one advantage to that is I won't have to jump in a bog, although I don't have any Easter eggs.

Chapter Four

There are Six of Us

Within ten miles of the RV park was one gas station and one dollar store. Both had been breached but not ransacked. Michael filled his pockets with cigarettes despite Jean saying he could load them in the SUV.

"Actually, Michael, you should really be off your feet. I can grab things for you."

Michael had not taken his shoes off until the shower, revealing the ugly reality of his migration. Both toenails of his big toes sloughed off the nail beds, and the blisters on the pads of his feet were like water balloons.

"How did you ..." Jean began, then covered her mouth.

Despite his obvious pain, Michael insisted on accompanying Jean on her survey of the local area. She offered to let Gunny stay with him and he refused.

"I don't wanna be alone," he said.

That settled things.

"What we really need is a map," Jean said, then pivoted to scan the parking lot where there were two abandoned trucks. "Maybe start checking glove compartments."

The gas station offered little to improve their situation, other than the cigarettes. The food was of the junk variety, although Jean did pause for a time at the sour cream and onion chips. She never forgot her purpose, the reunion she sought. But, with the Judith encounter followed shortly by meeting Gunny and then Michael ... she wondered if she was carving a new path, one that would take her away from them.

The sour cream and onion chips were undisturbed, meaning Henry and Penny had not visited that particular gas station. Maybe they drove right past it on their way to ...

Not the time to worry about it. The scent of cigarette smoke made her lungs itch. She missed it. She missed the heaviness in her chest, holding the smoke until it was painful. She stood by the window. Michael's back was to her. He wore an over-sized t-shirt with a roadrunner on the back, a college mascot Jean didn't recognize. Gunny sat beside him and eyed the parking lot as if Michael was the last sheep in his flock and there were wolves about. Michael exhaled a cloud of smoke and then swapped control of the cigarette to his left hand so his right was free to stroke Gunny's fur.

"You're a good boy. Are you a good boy?" Michael asked in his curious, childlike voice.

Jean wasn't sure her purpose if it wasn't finding Henry and Penny. Maybe that was okay. It was a new world now. The rules weren't carved in stone. She had time to figure things out.

The RV park was a good spot, especially after Jean removed all the signs directing people to it. And there *were* people over the next days and weeks. She didn't see them, but sometimes she heard them at night. Maybe it was the way sound traveled across the desert. Nothing to interrupt it save for a mesquite tree and an oil derrick trapped in time like a steel dinosaur. Distant engines. Gunfire once or twice. The headlights she saw at night could have been ten or two miles distant.

She did find a map and used it to eliminate possibilities regarding Henry and Penny's whereabouts, traveling county roads and surveying houses from a distance. Sometimes Gunny and Michael accompanied, but she mostly went alone. Jean returned to the RV before dark, surmising she surrendered fewer advantages in the day.

How quickly the extraordinary becomes routine. A stranger to the scene might have guessed Jean and Michael had lived in that RV with their miniature wolf all their lives. They ate well and spent most nights under the stars, now that Michael no longer feared them.

In early March, Jean embarked on a solo supply run, leaving Michael and Gunny at home to explore a new grocery store twenty miles to the west. Their oft-visited gas station was running low on Michael's favorites. Beyond cigarettes, that included chocolate bars with peanuts and any candy he could utilize as a straw. Jean also noticed there were items missing neither had taken. Someone passing through maybe, or a local survivor. If it was the latter, the fact they never encountered each other suggested he or she was cautious, which hopefully meant not a threat.

The grocery store was on the outskirts of a town that was small by most standards but large for the region. Before pulling into the lot, she parked behind a dumpster and watched for half an hour. It was that liminal space between seasons, where the sun could raise a sheen of sweat on your forehead that felt like frost at the slightest breeze. Jean leaned over the hood of the SUV, binoculars she pilfered from an abandoned truck pressed to her eyes as she debated retrieving her jacket.

This part of Texas was like a painting abandoned halfway through its creation. The colors were muted, yellowed grass bleached of its chlorophyll, brown mountains barren of trees and lacking any majesty. They were neither tall nor imposing, their peaks blunted by the rains from another epoch. What grew here huddled close to the roots dressed in spines or thorns, a warning to uninterested herbivores. Beneath the surface, the roots spoke. The old yucca recounting monsoons from seasons past.

There was little beauty to find, few colors to make the viewer wistful for a more vibrant version. Jean hoped other survivors would feel similarly disappointed and find no reason to linger.

The lot was vacant save for a few loose carts. Her SUV would stand out if she parked there. Instead, she checked her firearm, removed the binoculars, and sprinted across the road.

She buried her face in the crook of her elbow, the stench of rot wafting beyond the broken glass of the entrance door. Spoiled dairy, meat, and produce. It settled in the back of her throat like vomit half expelled. Thankfully, this was an exploratory journey, a quick inspection to understand the layout and search for signs of other visitors.

"Well, that's ..." Jean said, leaving the word *strange* unspoken.

The stench was strong and would have been worse had the offending goods not been removed from the shelves. What Jean smelled then was the essence, the residue that soaked into the ceiling tiles and carpets. Someone had been there, maybe more than one person. Maybe this was *their* store in the same way Jean thought of the gas station as hers.

Jean crouched behind a pyramid of potatoes, ear cocked and weapon ready. The memory of Marcus walking into the grocery store seemed like something she had seen on TV. That was how she *had* to think of it. It might have been a month ago by then, but already the details were fuzzy. Had Marcus looked over his shoulder, smiled and waved at her as he entered? Jean shook her head and emerged from her hiding place.

Grocery stores would not be around forever. Perhaps a second round of Stargazers would clean up the work undone by the first group. Maybe the tireless west Texas wind, hot as the air expelled from the lungs of a racehorse dying on the track, would be their end. While they did exist, her relationship to them would be like a deer to highway asphalt, haunted by the memory of dead kin.

Jean gathered Michael's essentials, expecting to see a face around every corner. The gun in her hand was as slick as a water moccasin and she had to repeatedly wipe sweat on her jeans. Halfway down the snacks aisle she stopped so suddenly her sneakers squeaked over the tiles. She kneeled then glanced to the left and right.

Some of the sour cream and onion chips were gone. Not all, but some. Jean smiled, picked up a bag and wondered if Penny might have held it previously. She would have wanted all of them. Henry would have told her they couldn't fill Ol' Reliable with just sour cream and onion chips. Misfit needed food, too. Penny would have agreed.

It was a fantasy, a projection of hope.

Hope, even misguided, felt a lot better in her heart than despair. She could live on hope for a while. For as long as it took.

Jean was still smiling as she sprinted across the parking lot and scaled the slight earthen incline to the dumpster. She turned the corner and skidded to a stop, the plastic bag slipping from her grasp.

There was a piece of paper on her windshield, held in place beneath the wiper blade. Jean dropped to a crouch, peered beneath the SUV.

"Hello?" she said in a voice she did not recognize as her own.

If there was someone close enough to hear her speak, they also heard the approach. Her hands were so sweaty the gun felt as if it had been dipped in oil. Jean duckwalked the five feet to the dumpster and peered inside.

"Shit," she mumbled and stood fully.

The lot, the store, and the desolate landscape around it were unchanged. Jean snatched the plastic bag and tossed it in the passenger's seat. She pocketed the paper and climbed inside the SUV. Her heart felt like a moth trapped in a lampshade. Someone saw her, had probably watched her as she surveyed the parking lot. They waited for her to leave.

She reversed, wrenched the steering wheel, and gunned it. Jean turned toward home, drove for two minutes and thought better of it. She checked her mirrors and sat taller in her seat. How had she been spotted? There were a few structures in the vicinity of the store, but none appeared occupied. A cell phone tower or one of the nearby mesas? Not likely. Her mystery witness would not have had time to scramble down, drive to the SUV, and leave without a trace in the time she was inside the store.

Jean turned down a dirt road on her right. Maybe they were still watching. Through binoculars, maybe a rifle scope.

She took another right turn.

"Goddammit," Jean whispered, checking her mirrors again. The SUV was trailed by a cloud of dust half a mile long. If she was still being watched she might as well have lights and sirens on. She needed to get back to asphalt. She eased to a stop and turned the SUV around.

Jean squinted and flipped the visor down, the sun inching toward the soft teeth of the old mountains. She didn't know the road she was on, and there was nothing to distinguish one mesa from another. She would need to use the map to find her way home, so she stopped again and put the SUV in park. The justification for her panic was fully dependent on the intentions of the note writer.

The paper partially tore as she pulled it from her pocket. She licked her lips and oriented herself to the thin, wispy calligraphy.

She read the note, read it again, then reclined in her seat.

"Well, that's somethin'."

"What took you so long?" Michael asked, the unlit cigarette in his fingers wrinkled, the paper overworked.

"Sorry," Jean said, holding the bag out as a peace offering. "It was a ... different sort of trip."

Gunny licked her hand as Michael took the bag.

"No cigarettes?" he said.

Jean chuckled, "I think it would take you about another year to go through what we got."

Michael nodded, face lighting up at the sight of the candy.

"After dinner. And you'll brush your teeth as soon as you're done."

Michael frowned and dropped the bag between his legs.

"So, what took so long?" he asked again.

"Did you let Gunny go potty while I was gone?"

He shook his head, "I don't like going outside when you're not here."

Jean motioned for him to follow, "Let's go talk about it."

Gunny nearly took her legs out as he bolted toward his favorite bush. Its wilted leaves indicated it did not appreciate his daily blessings. Michael emerged, lit cigarette pasted to his lips with a lungful of smoke ready to exhale.

"So yeah, I went to the big grocery store, the one we saw before. It's got a lot of stuff on the shelves, but I don't think I was the only shopper. I know I wasn't. I grabbed your stuff and, oh yeah, there was some sour cream chips missin' so that might be good news," Jean said with a wink. "Anyway, I left the store plannin' to head back here and I found a note on the windshield."

Michael often blinked in absence of commentary, shifting his weight from one foot to the next, flicking ashes. Jean smoothed the paper and squinted at the wispy letters. They were difficult to read, but she already memorized the message.

"There are six of us. One doctor. We have a safe place, lots of food, and quite the story to tell. Little league fields at five o'clock. Neutral territory if you want to meet. Bring your dog ☺ "

Jean folded the note and Michael nodded, blinking and inhaling. She didn't share the postscript, the warning about others in the area. The suggestion to stay off the roads at night.

"We gonna go?" Michael asked.

Jean shrugged, "We could check it out from a distance. See what they look like first."

Michael nodded liberated another cigarette from the pack.

"Oh, and there was somethin' else. I got kinda spooked from the note, thought someone might be following me. So, I took the long way home. Got into some territory we haven't checked out yet. There was a red light, like one of those fireworks the kids hold even though they're not supposed to? You know, the tube that shoots out the different colors?"

"I like fireworks," Michael said, eyes drifting to the stars.

"Me too, Michael."

Jean nudged the ground with her toe sending the rocking chair back a few inches. The chair, borrowed from the porch of a nearby farmhouse, reminded her of one from her grandma's old home. It didn't feel the same to sit in it. Her feet didn't reach the floor back then. The motion was familiar, however, like the push and pull of the ocean near the shore.

In the RV, Michael slept with an arm around Gunny. His snore was like a white noise machine set to *static*. A click-clack of nails indicated the dog tolerated the arrangement for only a few minutes before extricating himself and seeking a less crowded space. Some mornings, Jean found Michael nestled against Gunny at the foot of the bed, having reversed his position during the night.

After dinner that evening, Jean directed Michael to go inside the RV, explaining what she planned to do without fully articulating the rationale.

"Cover Gunny's ears Michael. Hopefully will only take one shot."

It did. The streetlight exploded in a flare of sparks. Two seconds later, Jean stood in total darkness as glass drizzled over the gravel.

"Well, shit," she whispered, pivoting to the right and quickly losing her sense of direction.

There was a faint strip of light leaking through a gap between the blinds and the side of a window frame of the RV. Jean walked toward it with her hands outstretched. Each step felt like it was over open air, as if she might plummet into nothing. Still, she couldn't risk being discovered. Whatever the letter writer's aim, her anxiety spiked knowing she was not alone.

"Everything's okay, Michael. Just gotta use a flashlight if you go out at night," Jean said upon entering the RV.

"But why'd you shoot it? We can't see now," Michael said, peeking through the blinds.

"Yep. We can't see and we're less likely to be seen. Remember what I told you happened in that town? Remember about Marcus and that man at the motel? For you and me this Stargazer stuff was the worst thing that could happen. We lost everything. But for some people, people like the man in the grocery store and the monster in the motel, they get to be proud about how bad they're broken. Ain't nobody to tell 'em they're sick or lock 'em up. There's just folks like you and me, hopefully a lot more of us than them. We're too busy tryin' to make it. Aren't we Gunny?" Jean said, massaging the dog's ear with a knuckle.

Michael found he enjoyed using the flashlight to pee and had no further questions. He fought sleep as usual and succumbed to it about ten minutes after yawning through an exclamation of *I'm not tired!*

Jean nudged the ground again. She shook a cigarette free from its pack, sniffed its unlit end. Why not have a smoke? If this wasn't the end of the world, she could pass the threshold to it at any time. Saliva filled her mouth. Memories of cigarettes after a good meal. Paired with a beer after a hard day at work. Why not?

She tucked the cigarette into its pack and craned her neck skyward. It was a view she learned to love all over again, one that made her feel both insignificant and extraordinary. For so many, the stars were among the last things they saw. Then came the destruction, the violence. The walking, seemingly without pur-pose. Jean's eyes traced lines between the stars of a constellation she forgot the name of, settling on the brightest.

"I told you I wouldn't. That's why," Jean said, eyes misting. "But if you want to relieve me of that oath, just give me a sign."

The chair mouse squeaked with every rock. But the sound was preferable to silence. It was so dark the stars felt like the peaks of diamond tipped waves viewed from the depths.

"Actually, any sign right now would be just fine by me."

Apocalypse Radio

I think the Stargazers are done. I've heard from about half the states, a couple provinces and some folks in the Caribbean. No reports of Stargazers since the third week of February. Maybe there were a few that went unobserved. I suppose it doesn't matter now. If there were a handful back in February, there are none today. So, what do we with that information? It's just us now. No chance of Mom or Dad, lovers or friends coming to their senses, knocking on your door or tapping a stick on the entrance to your cave.

With the few exceptions I noted previously, we are alone. We are the present end of our genetic line. Everyone you loved is dead, but **you** are still here.

Why?

Why are you here? Why am **I** here? That's the question for now. For today. For this month. For as long as you need. Find an answer to that question. Find it before your next move. Without it, how will you face what comes next?

If there was debate about the origin of our downfall, by that I mean I read many posts suggesting this was natural, a pandemic

...

That perspective does not stand up against the reality of the new additions to our fair land. The caller from Carolina called back and clarified what she saw. Not that it makes much more sense even with the new details. And she's not alone. I don't know if *monument* is the appropriate descriptor. But there are others now. Other reports coming in. One from Illinois and another from Utah. They're massive, apparently, and hard to describe.

I read a book maybe fifteen years ago. It talked about what would happen to the planet if humans disappeared. How long would it take for New York to become a forest again? Surprisingly, not long. According to that book, it was the monuments that would last the longest. Not all of them. Think Rushmore. I don't know if that logic is connected to this, just a thought.

One of my last posts, before the web finally collapsed, hinted at the source of our current plight. They were all lookin' to the skies, weren't they? Seems reasonable to believe there was somethin' to that. I think I compared it to moving into a new house, hiring an exterminator to eliminate the pests. But what if the pests could do most of the work? What if they could destroy their own nests?

That's our world now. We've destroyed most of our nests. Maybe the ones out in the yard you don't really notice unless you go lookin' for 'em aren't of immediate concern. Maybe they never will be.

Still, it's only good for a little while. Pests find a way, don't they? Knock over a tub of sugar and see how many were hidin' in the walls. We don't know what that looks like for us. Our tub of sugar. What could it be? I don't know. Just keep your wits about you as things change.

As I said, that's our world now. Don't know what's above us, but we can guess part of the intent by what's been done already. They've eliminated the pests. Are they movin' in? Are they flippin' the house? Just thinkin' about the possibilities makes my guts turn to soup.

I ask again, why are you here? Was it an accident? Should you have done like they did? Led your children into the sea, jumped off a bridge? Walked into a human inferno? Beyond survivin' another day, why did you get out of bed this morning, or roll out of your sleepin' bag?

I don't know the answer for myself. But maybe, talkin' with you I'll find it.

The borders are gone. Isn't that wild? Just like that. (snaps fingers) There is no America or Canada. No Mexico. No anthems or flags. There's just you, and me, and this beautiful world to explore. Maybe that's reason enough.

(sighs)

It's funny. I used to read fantasy. I would study the maps in those books as if I was gonna be quizzed on it. I imagined myself on an adventure. A quest. Murky forests thick with spiders. Deserts and mountains, cold lakes black as oil. Well, it's all out there now. I guess I just need a quest.

On the lighter side of the news, there are reports out of Texas, what *was* Texas I guess, of a small herd of elephants moving west away from the ruins of San Antonio. If you're travelin' out that way, maybe consider leavin' some peanuts on the road. That's a thing, isn't it? Peanuts and elephants?

Thinkin' about it now, I should probably have shared this before the elephants. End on a good note, right? Can't verify this account. I hope it's just someone havin' a little fun. Wrong kinda fun considerin' the state of the world if you ask me. There was a note left in a mailbox off I-80 in Nebraska. West of where Lincoln used to be, I believe. Fellow radio enthusiast found it. Took a picture of it–guess cell phones are still good for that. Put it back in the mailbox in case, like I said, it's true. Made contact with me shortly after.

The note was unsigned, but the author claims there are people huntin' other people for sport. Mostly off the interstate, sounds like.

(sighs)

Not just that. They're takin' trophies. Ears, eyes, fingers. Displaying the bodies as well. (clears throat) Turned one man into a scarecrow, of sorts. His, uh, manhood was in his left hand, and there was a hat in the right. Handful of pennies in it. There was a younger ... uh ... well, there are other victims.

If you're headin' that direction, I'd suggest you stay far off the interstate.

(sighs)

Sounds like these monsters know why they're here. If you're still wondering for yourself, don't wonder too long.

CHAPTER FIVE

ARE YOU OKAY?

"See anyone?" Michael asked. From their position over-looking the town, the buildings and trees blended together. The latter browned in the middle stages of a slow death, the irrigation that sustained them no longer providing.

"Not yet. Think we missed Daylight Saving Time?" Jean chuckled. When Michael did not respond, she dropped the binoculars and cocked an eyebrow. His lips formed an O, tongue like a curious salamander stabbing through the middle of it. He exhaled smoke, which failed to form the ring he anticipated.

"That's not how–" Jean began. "Michael, you don't have to stick your tongue out to do it."

He frowned, then pulled a cigarette from the pack and offered it to her.

"Show me?"

She took the cigarette as if it was a sleeping hornet that might rouse at the slightest disturbance.

"I told you about Marcus, right? About the promise I made?"

Michael shrugged, "I promised Mama I would quit smokin' every day. I meant it when I said it, but ..."

He took a second drag, opened his mouth wide and exhaled another disappointing cloud. Did it count as smoking if she was just teaching Michael how to blow rings? Marcus would have thought so and said nothing about it. Instead, his eyebrows would arch toward his hairline like brown caterpillars abandoning a hot sidewalk. Paired with that smirk that was somehow both a frown and a smile at once, there was no need to speak to it.

"Michael, I don't know—"

He grabbed her shoulder and spun her around, pointing at the baseball field maybe half a mile distant.

"Oh, shit," Jean said, leaning over the hood with her eyes pressed to the binoculars.

"Whaddya see?"

"Oh, not much. I mean, there's people, but they're all blurry. Looks to be two right now. Can't tell if man or woman."

Gunny sat up in the front seat, his hot breath immediately fogging the windshield. Perhaps the slight shift in Jean's tone cut through the muted, watercolor haze of his dream. She noticed him in her peripheral vision.

"Give Gunny some love, will ya? And don't blow smoke in his face, please."

Michael was happy to oblige. In the past few weeks, petting Gunny seemed to be second to only smoking for Michael's favorite thing.

"There's another comin'."

"We goin' to meet 'em?"

Jean sucked her teeth, "No, I don't think so. I guess if they'd wanted to, they could've ambushed me in the store. Must not have wanted to. But they are strangers and I haven't had the best of luck with them."

She placed the binoculars next to the gun on the hood of the SUV, then twisted her torso forcing her spine to pop. Michael, who was halfway into the passenger seat, emerged, blinking as if he was staring at the sun.

"That sounded like Mama's farts," he said, shifted in place for a few seconds, then resumed petting Gunny.

Jean was too stunned to laugh, and instead coughed in rapid fire succession, and her eyes watered from the effort. Half a minute passed before she collected herself enough to bark, "Did you just make a joke?"

Michael shrugged, "I guess if you think it's funny. It just sounded like farts to me. Mama farted all the time. She said it was 'cause she ate so many salads at work and they gave her the bubbles. But I seen what she snuck out of her jobs, and it wasn't ever salad."

"I'm gonna remember that one, Michael. And it's good to know I can fart around you."

"Gunny does it."

Jean chuckled and retrieved the binoculars.

"Uh oh."

There were three of them on the baseball field, one on the far right clearly pointing her direction.

"They can't see us. Can they?" she whispered.

The SUV was hidden behind a leafy, evergreen shrub. The tallest branches were over six feet, half a foot taller than the vehicle's roof. They were also situated on an incline. There was no way the strangers could see them. The branches twitched with wind but did not sway. There were no gaps among them. A reflection off the binoculars?

"They're ... they're wavin' at us."

Gunny plopped down in his seat, a halo of hair encircling him. Michael dusted his hands off and stood beside Jean.

"We should meet 'em," he said.

"We don't *know* them, Michael. They could be anybody."

Michael plucked another cigarette from his pack but paused before lighting it. He scratched the patch of scruff growing in the hollow of his cheek, light brown like a tuft of summer grass beyond the reach of the water sprinkler.

"Ain't we anybody to them?" he said.

It was true. Save for Michael and the two people she hoped were somewhere nearby, Jean had no friends in this new world, no allies. Every person she met would be a stranger. Presuming ill intent would erode her prospects for survival, and Michael's. Sooner than she might like to imagine, the shelves would be purged of anything decent. What then? She'd never killed anything bigger than a squirrel, and that was an accident that infected her dreams for months afterward.

"I suppose we are. It just ... feels too soon. There's gonna be some kind of structure to the world. Don't have a guess what that might be. The bad folks will sort themselves out, 'cause you can't survive long with the devil in ya. Not talkin' about the bible, either. I just mean those intent on causin' chaos expose themselves to chaos. And a lot can go wrong. They gotta be perfect every time. Always. Good guys like us just have to be lucky once."

Michael's gaze drifted as Jean spoke, as if following the flight pattern of a bird only he could see. Sometimes Jean talked to herself while looking at him. He nodded a bit, but there was no understanding in his eyes. Jean's hands moved a lot when she spoke, which gave him something to look at. She flicked her hand toward the baseball fields, and he followed the direction she indicated. Michael's glazed-over expression hardened. He slid a cigarette between his lips and pointed.

"The best thing to do right now is to wait ..." Jean said, trailing off as she recognized the approaching shapes for what they were. "Oh, shit!"

The last non-Stargazers Jean interacted with were Henry and Penny. Weeks ago? Had it been a month? It was easy to believe she and Michael were alone, the rare, distant rumble of an engine a memory stirred by silence rather than heard.

She snatched her gun off the hood and nudged Michael, "Get in! We're leaving!"

"But–"

"Hurry Michael!"

The SUV roared to life. She threw it in gear and sprayed rocks across the asphalt leaving rubber behind, fishtailing a couple heartbeats before finding traction.

"Sorry guys!" Jean said, bracing Gunny with one arm while fighting the steering wheel with the other. In the backseat, Michael was like a turtle tipped on its shell, the cigarette broken but still glued to his bottom lip.

She checked the rearview mirror just before a turn put the area of their surveillance out of sight. The strangers stood in the disturbed earth her tires carved through only moments before. She fixated on one man, a head taller than the others with silver hair like tinsel stripped of its shine, who waved at her. He wore no shirt, and Jean thought it was not warm enough for that choice. Though he likely couldn't see her, and despite everything she told Michael about avoiding strangers, she waved back.

Michael calmed down after a cigarette, which Jean let him smoke with his head out the window.

"I'm like Gunny!" he said, tongue like a strip of taffy.

Jean eased to a stop in the highway, eyes bouncing between the map and the environment. From some angles, and with the right lighting, the land was beautiful. Not frequently, and never for long. As the sun set, the mesas shed their brown shells for campfire umber, rose dusted pink. The mesquite that looked like the charred innards of a mastodon under the glare of the sun became alien sculptures. It was the desert attempting to mask its hidden terrors just before dark, to lull the sun-warmed prey to linger on the surface a moment longer.

"I think it was around here," Jean said, chin grazing the top of the steering wheel.

"Huh?"

"The fireworks?"

The term was not a precise match for what Jean witnessed that night, but it painted the clearest picture in Michael's mind.

"Oh yeah," he yawned, head resting against the window glass.

"When we were stuck in the motel, before everything happened with Judith, Henry and I talked about what we would do if we got separated. I guess we didn't think it would happen so soon, 'cause we never got past the idea of leavin' signs. Maybe that was a sign. I'd like to find out where it came from, at least. I can scope it out from a distance."

"Okay," Michael offered as his hand snaked around the passenger seat like a blind spider. It settled in Gunny's fur.

Jean folded the map and sighed, "I don't think it was this dark out. Maybe that doesn't matter, but I kinda think it does. We should probably head home, maybe try again tomorrow. I don't think the strangers followed me, but they for sure know which direction we came from."

"Okay."

"You gonna say anything besides *okay*?" Jean asked.

"Alright."

She laughed, "Fair enough. Let's get home and see what kinda gourmet meal we can dump out of a can tonight."

After a handful of seconds, the purpose for the excursion at the forefront of her thoughts, Jean said, "I worry they kept goin', maybe all the way to New Mexico or somewhere with water. We used words like *close* or *near* when talkin' about an unplanned separation but didn't really define what it meant."

"Mmhmm," Michael offered.

"They shoulda caught up to your group, though. Michael, do you remember any vehicles passin' by while you were walkin'?"

He sighed, "Yeah, when it first started. Some of them attacked the star people. Ran 'em over or shot at 'em. I got scared when I heard an engine, tried to make myself small."

"Do you remember what they, what the cars looked like?"

Michael issued long, steady breaths, then said, "I didn't look. I was scared to."

The tone of his voice shifted, the sadness he typically reserved for late night philosophical questions about heaven creeping into his words. Ol' Reliable was an uncommon vehicle, big and boxy, the paint the color of autumn leaves you wouldn't go out of your way to notice. It was a relic, glossy only when it rained. Still, Michael recalling it would not change her circumstances. They might have been headed west only to turn due north after passing Michael's group. It was more likely one of the new strangers knew of a man traveling with his daughter and a small dog with panda colors, which influenced the calculus in her mind regarding her relationship to them.

"Guess we can try a new spot tomorrow. Thought it was here, though, or close to it. Don't fall asleep, Michael, or you'll be up all night."

Michael grunted in response. Jean drove, eyes darting to the rearview every few seconds hoping to see a sign, a repeat of the previous evening. Within a minute, Michael's drool slimed a snail trail on the window. He snored like a cartoon character pretending to sleep.

She turned onto a familiar street and navigated home without consulting the map. Her hand reached for the radio on instinct, but she didn't turn it on. The static was a reminder of the music she would never hear again. Despite the total absence of traffic, Jean adhered to stop signs, unable to overcome thirty-five years of compliance as a driver.

She braced Gunny as she eased to a stop. He opened one eye, then the other. The growl in his throat was like a Harley idling a block away. He sat up, ears ironed flat to his skull, hair rising like a mane around his head.

Jean was looking at Gunny, not the twin cones of light stabbing the intersection ahead and the desert beyond. It came running out of the darkness at a full sprint, leapt over the hood and crashed through the windshield.

Its foot, studded with desert debris, hovered an inch from Jean's nose. She screamed, threw her hands up and hit the gas. The new passenger reclaimed its leg, scoring trenches in the flesh. Gunny erupted, spittle pebbling the fractured windshield. Michael cried out from the backseat as the SUV soared through the intersection and crashed onto the uneven desert terrain. Tires fought for purchase and the vehicle rocked like a buoy unmoored. Gunny mashed his nose to the windshield as the passenger on the hood re-oriented itself.

Jean melted into her seat, arms like twin saplings trembling under a hurricane's wind. She drove blindly and unaware, the figure corrupting her view. It was human, having all the necessary components to qualify. It was also unnatural, a ghoul half-formed in a nightmare. Its hair, wispy like cotton stuffing leaking from an old pillow sparkled with glass shards. The skin of its face was gray-white like a mushroom, like something grown in the dark.

Jean's legs stiffened, the gas pedal mashed to the floor as she recoiled from the head peeking through the hole in the windshield. The eyes were glazed, albino grapes painted with lacquer, a foggy, dark color at their center. Michael rolled into a ball, screams leaking through the seam between his forearm and biceps. Gunny's claws gouged the dashboard, teeth like little white daggers gnashing air.

This was not a Stargazer. Nor was it human. Maybe a human who resisted, one who came part of the way back to himself. A hybrid, something between. Maybe it was her future, Michael's too. It felt as though Jean's muscles disconnected from her skeleton, the sinew as soft as Gunny's fur.

What if she and Michael didn't survive? What if they only delayed a different form of torture? It breeched the windshield, glass glittering like desert sand catching moonlight.

"Mama! Mamaaa!" Michael cried, then added, "Jean!"

Gunny lunged, seizing the barely-there skin of one cheek and bumping the steering wheel.

Time slowed. The SUV careened, front passenger tire colliding with a stone, that for the previous million years had only ever served to provide a bit of shade for desert insects. The vehicle flipped, the hood's passenger arching into the air, a strip of ghost flesh pinched between Gunny's teeth left behind.

Glass shattered. Metal shrieked. The SUV tumbled, two of its occupants not restrained by seatbelts rolling like anti-static balls in a dryer. The steering wheel airbag deployed as the momentum of the cartwheeling vehicle pulled Jean's face to within inches of it. Her head snapped back and she saw an explosion of white, a supernova collapsing to a pinpoint. Then her senses closed in one by one.

Still, they rolled, the SUV's skeleton losing structural integrity with each revolution. Jean reached for her new family, vision fading. Michael went limp, limbs no longer bracing against the impact. Gunny, by chance, wedged between the front and rear seats. His growl softened to a whine, thoughts of defending his family abandoned in a moment of self-preservation. The white fur of his face was speckled with blood, though not his own. He showed teeth but there was no aggression in the display.

And then it stopped, halfway to righting itself, the SUV crashed onto its side dragging all occupants toward the desert floor.

The figure, like a Halloween decoration come to life, stood on twisted legs. Had Jean been conscious to see, she would have classified it as something other than a Stargazer. Something different. Something new.

The back of its skull nearly grazed the spine. Its mouth opened wide as if hoping to swallow the moon. Instead, it belched a bauble of amber light. Once ejected, the body collapsed, black blood squelching from wounds new and old.

The light circled the hissing wreck for a few seconds, flirted with entry. Though not guided by intellect, a decision was made and it floated away, an ember caught in an updraft.

Michael was aware of the cold first. He blinked at the open window, tatters of glass lining its border. Beyond it was the night sky, constellations with names he could not remember no matter how many times Jean told him.

Jean.

He grabbed the nearest headrest and pulled.

"Ouch!" he seethed, glass biting into the pads of his fingers.

"Jean?"

No response. He turned his ear toward the window, heard the subtle pitter-patter of liquid drizzling over the desert floor. And something else, a breath punctuated by a click.

"Gunny?"

A paw was visible, resting on the center console. Michael reached for it, gave it a squeeze. Still warm. That was good.

He knew it would hurt, but he grasped the headrest again and pulled himself up until he was in a crouching posture. Whatever attacked the vehicle was either dead or gone. Michael only glimpsed it for a moment, but that was enough.

"Ouch!" he barked upon putting pressure on his left ankle. Other injuries announced themselves, cuts and bruises, ligaments extended beyond their limits.

He screamed as something wet and warm grazed the top of his hand. Then he saw the face, Gunny straining to peak beyond Jean's seat.

"Gunny! Are you okay boy?"

The dog licked more urgently, flinging spittle, grunting, claws digging into the cushioned surface of the console.

"Hold on, Gunny. Lemme get out first, and then I can help you."

Using Jean's seat, the console, then the passenger seat as steps, Michael climbed out of the window with no further injuries. He stood, the broken window between his open legs, and wrenched the front passenger door open. Gunny wriggled in his seat, reversing the position of his head and hindquarters.

"Oh boy," Michael mumbled, gauging the distance between his feet and the desert floor. Even if he dropped down safely there was the matter of the one-hundred-pound dog. As if to eliminate the consternation, Gunny removed himself from the equation, scrambling up his seat and bounding out the SUV's open door.

"Are you okay?" Michael called.

Gunny stood, walked in a circle, and pissed on a shrub.

Michael rubbed his hands together and squatted over the passenger seat. The airbag was deflated, pooled to the side where Jean lay hidden behind her arms. Her chest rose and fell, and that was good. Michael patted the place on his own chest where he normally stored his cigarettes. That shirt had no pocket there, however.

She was breathing, which meant she was alive. But there was a hitching quality to it, a rattle at the peak of the breath. He didn't like the sound, the way her body shuddered as if the airway was pinched. Michael lowered himself to one knee, reached an arm inside and groped blindly. His cold-numbed hand prodded the fabric of her shirt. Despite the tingle in his fingers, he sensed the moisture.

"Oh no," he said, and wiped the blood on his jeans.

It was night now, and nothing looked familiar. He was alone, in a desert, and he feared Jean was dying.

Apocalypse Radio

I t's not my intent to become the conspiracy platform for our times, the end times feels like. It's not productive. It brings us no closer to normalcy, to the community I referred to a couple weeks ago. Bad information, even offered with the best intentions, is poisonous. Once you commit to chasin' phantoms ... well, you better get used to the sight of an empty net.

I spoke with a man from Montana. Lives on a ranch an hour from the nearest population center. Get the sense he was a bit of a prepper. Wasn't ... excited about the state of the world, but he also wasn't disturbed by it. Seemed like he thought this was inevitable.

(sighs)

I hesitate to recount our conversation in full. I did record it, but the improvements to my audio set up can't account for a twang that thick. I've spent the majority of my life in and around the sticks but still had trouble keepin' up. Think he was just excited to have someone to talk to. Could be the first conversation he had since it all went down.

His theory must have been like, like a ten-ton weight on his shoulders. Like the world's shiniest penny, and he had no one to show it to. If it's real ... if it's real, it changes everything in a way I can't quite grasp. Not yet. Suffice it to say, his theory and mine are not the same. I suppose if we shine a harsh enough light on 'em we might see some overlap, but on the surface it's apples and oranges.

That word, *if*, is big enough to fill a room, though.

(silence)

I'm ... I'm drinkin' tonight, friends. You'll have to forgive me if my words get furry.

Y'all know what I meant when I mentioned lookin' to the skies for answers, right? Can I go ahead and say the word now? Aliens? It made the most sense to me even though I didn't understand *how* it could've happened. I mean, conceptually, I have an idea. But I don't know the mechanics of it. The execution.

(swallows, sighs)

At what point would you consider mankind advanced? When we built the megaliths? When we learned how to fight disease? How about when we landed on the moon, or when we started blowin' shit up harnessin' the power of the atom? Whatever you believe, it's been pretty recent ... in a cosmological sense. Even the fastest burnin' stars still burn for millions of years. I mean, there's trees on this planet that were mature when most people were hunter/gatherers, usin' leaves as toilet paper.

Come to think of it, our current process isn't that far off. Leaves and toilet paper I mean.

(silence)

I'm … I'm ramblin' folks, and I apologize for it. I'm sure there are people better suited to this task I created for myself, bein' the world's last DJ. Who am I anyway? Why should you listen to a goddamned word I …

(sighs, bottle uncorks followed by the sound of pouring liquid)

It made sense to look up. We're a young species. If you buy the science, we've only been around a few hundred thousand years. Go further back than that and we're less recognizable as human. But look what we did in that time, what we achieved in the past century. What if modern humans had been around one million years ago? Ten million? A billion? Assumin' we didn't kill ourselves first, where would our technology be?

If you believe there is intelligent life beyond our planet, it ain't a stretch to imagine some, or maybe many of them did have a head start. I mean, our best telescopes could see back almost 14 billion years …

So, it kinda made sense these … beings, this intelligence could, from a distance, interact with our minds, with the gray matter in our skulls. Why not? It's remote-control technology, isn't it? Only, the remote didn't work on everyone. A faulty receiver maybe. Coulda been part of the plan. Who knows.

Yeah, it made sense in a way this new possibility, well, I'm gonna have to sit with it for a while. If you're willing to entertain my ramblin' a bit longer, I'll begin wrappin' up with this …

If it's true, we'd be better served lookin' back than lookin' up. Back in time. What in our recorded past, in the stories before recordin' was a possibility, looks like today? I don't mean the Stargazers. I mean the world they left behind. The ruins of mankind's hubris. That the right word? Hubris? Never felt comfortable usin' it in conversation. Thought I'd make a fool of myself to someone much smarter than me.

We've been here before, folks. Humanity dancin' on a knife's edge, our technology impossible to replicate among our few and fractured numbers.

...

...

We're headed back to the stone age. The batteries bridgin' us to our not-distant past will corrode. I'm not sure how many potatoes it would take to power this thing, but I don't have any right now. Guess I better get to plantin'.

I'll leave you with this thought. When times are tough, and that's a hell of an understatement to describe our current situation, where do you turn? Where do you think *they* turned? Our few and fractured ancestors...the ones who emerged from their hidin' places blinkin' dust from their eyes, starin' at the sky that betrayed them?

It's a lot to consider. Like I said, I don't want my voice to be associated with the poison of a sugar-coated lie. My challenge to you is ... if you're readin' the tea leaves in your cup properly, think about how you might go about things differently if it's not aliens. If it's somethin' from our past.

No fun news to pass along, I'm afraid. I hope those elephants are doin' okay.

Chapter Six

We Have Much to Discuss

The ocean, the black sea recedes, and in its place is static, electricity sparking in her extremities. Like her blood cells have been spiked with broken glass. Part of her longs for the deep, a great black nothing outside of memory or pain, the possibility of future suffering. It is a perfectly balanced place on the periphery of a dream. Part of her feels she has a choice, to sink down and down. To open her mouth and breathe, inhale the darkness. Fill her lungs with it.

The sea foam leaves words on the shore, names.

Michael

Penny

Henry

It is most painful near the shore, away from the uncaring void.

She has already made this choice. There will be a time for darkness, a time to forget. But it is not now.

"Michael?" Jean squeaked.

Her mind was an anchor, limbs and senses orbiting around it outside her control.

Concentrate on your breathing.

She visualized air traveling through her nostrils and into her lungs, holding there for a moment before reversing course. One breath. Two. Pressure across her eyes, and a dull pain that intensified in concert with her heartbeat. Fabric beneath the fingertips of her left hand. She redirected her focus, fingers twitching but not under her control. She attempted the same effort with her right hand but could not feel the fabric, as if her fist was a mallet.

Her tongue peeked between her lips and became stuck there. How would she look if there was someone in the room with her? Fingers twitching, tongue stuck to her upper lip. And there might be. Jean hadn't pushed past the pain to attempt opening her eyes. The thought of being watched unleashed a flurry of questions. Who would watch her, and where was she? Her last memory was of the wraith on the hood, the skin peeling from its calf like gray butter.

Was she in the SUV? No. She was on a flat surface, head slightly elevated by a pillow or something similar. She had been removed from the SUV while unconscious. Transported. There was no breeze, though. No sense of sunlight on her cheeks. She was inside … somewhere. Had been relocated there. By Michael? The recollection of his scream was so abrupt and stark in her mind he could have been standing beside her then.

"Michael?" she whispered.

There was a voice nearby, alternating between singing and humming. If she was in a house, it might have been in an adjoining room. But there was an underwater quality to it, as though cotton plugged her ears. Maybe a second voice? Jean sat up, a reflex. Her left hand prodded the space around her. A small table to the side and nothing else of interest. She shook her right arm, attempting to force feeling into her hand. Instead, it felt as if she shoved her hand into a colony of fire ants. She seethed, gritted her teeth.

Jean peeled a blanket off her body and eased one leg over the edge of a bed. Her bare foot touched cool tiles.

"Michael?" she said, a little louder, an ear cocked toward the sound of humming.

She planted her right foot beside the left.

"Goddamnit," she whispered, trying and failing to stand and open her eyes. The pressure and pain kept that instinct at bay.

What if she was dead? Or dying in the SUV? Marcus used to read books about near-death experiences. He got so animated when recounting the stories. Jean would nod and allow her mind to drift to that place it went to when she wasn't terribly interested in what Marcus had to say. Usually, it was something about football or that elf game he played with his friends, the one with the ridiculous die. The near-death memories were generally, but not exclusively pleasant, a sense of peace and light, voices of loved ones beckoning. Some experiencers reported glimpses of a place that could only be hell, but Jean dismissed these, both paths actually, as a final courtesy between the brain and the dying body that hosted it, or revenge.

Was there a mention of utter darkness? Of a hand that refused to respond to the demands of its owner? Jean rocked forward and stood, fingers of her left hand closing around air.

"Goddamnit!" she hissed.

BRRTTT

Jean balled her left hand into a fist, brandished it at nothing, then sniffed several times.

"Gunny?" she said, sweeping a leg in front of her. "Gunny, is that you?"

A scrabbling of nails over tiles, then his head burrowed into her belly. He whined, pressing harder, paw slapping her thigh. He must have been asleep beside the bed. Jean kneeled. Though Gunny wasn't much of a licker, he blessed her chin several times, his whine rising in urgency.

"It's okay, Gunny. It's okay."

She petted him with her left hand as the right arm was still on fire.

"It's okay!" she said, angling her chin away.

Jean felt the sensation of crying, but no tears streaked her cheeks. As she realized this, she also noticed the voice was quiet. She shifted to her knees, gripped the bed and huddled against it.

"Shhh ..." she said, failing to quiet Gunny's whines.

Footsteps. The air pressure in the room shifted, and she knew she was not alone. What if she had to fight her way out? She still couldn't see, hand only one good hand for the moment.

"Jean?"

Her breath hitched in her lungs. She relaxed her grip on the bed and emerged from behind it.

"Michael?"

If it was possible to sprint in three steps, Michael did so then. Jean was washed in his familiar scents, cigarette smoke and apple shampoo. He hoisted her to her feet and allowed his neck to droop over her shoulder.

"I was scared ... you ..." he sniffed.

"I was scared, too."

It was at that moment she knew she was not dead, not rewarded with a final vision of peace before passing. She never felt love in a dream like she did for that young man, for the dog clutching her leg with two paws.

"But, Michael, how did you ... and why can't I see?"

A man cleared his throat. One of the underwater voices spoke to her clearly from across the room, "I believe I can answer your questions, Jean. How about we get you some water and maybe a bite to eat first? Oh, and you can call me Doc."

They returned Jean to the bed she abandoned only moments before. Though this time Michael and Gunny joined her, the latter wedging between her legs and resting his head on her belly. She drank water, stomach stretching until it was just shy of painful. While she ate dried fruit (doctor's orders, as it was impossible to chew quickly), she realized there were fewer teeth in her mouth. That injury would soon be forgotten when she learned the extent of the others.

"We couldn't save the hand. Too much time had passed without adequate blood flow," Doc said.

"I'm sorry Jean I tried to find 'em quick as I could, but it was dark, and it all looked the same ..." Michael began.

Jean rubbed Michael's back with her remaining hand. "You saved my life from the sound of it. I guess that makes us even."

"He found his way back to the baseball fields and started screaming there. Walked toward town and screamed until Lucy heard him. Hard part after that was finding our way back to you, but Michael was helpful. There's only so many intersections that look like the one he described. To be honest, Jean, I might not have been able to save it even with a surgical suite and a team of technicians. It's not my specialty and it was probably best just to stop the blood loss."

Jean nodded, held the stump in the air as if she could see it. "My eyes?"

Doc inhaled before he spoke, "Also not my specialty, but I'm hopeful. I've seen impact injuries like this before. When they show up in my office, I refer them to El Paso or San Antonio. You wouldn't believe how many people around here have been taken out by cows, or steers. I guess I never learned the difference. I can't give you a number. Every injury is different. I'll just say I'm hopeful."

They sat in silence as Jean considered how unfair that word was. *Hopeful.*

"Where did you take me to?" she asked.

"You're at my place. It's a bit outside of town, if you can call it that. Where the town was, I should say."

"Who are the others? The people you were with?"

Doc waited so long to respond Jean nearly asked the question a second time.

"Complicated. One survivor like you. The others are, well, let's just say there's a lot more to that story, but it's not my story to tell. Lucy is a local. Or was. Sorry, I don't know if I'll ever get my tenses right. We knew each other in passing. You know, small towns and all. She worked at a hotel and would tell you there's nothing special about her. Doesn't quite understand why she's here and almost no one else is. I'll tell you she's right about most things, but not that. She's out on a supply run but will introduce herself if you're still awake when she returns."

"The others? The other people you were with?" Jean said, and when he did not respond, followed it up with, "Doc?"

"I know we just met, and under pretty awful circumstances. You have no reason to trust what I've told you is true. I hope the fact Michael is here and taken care of will be a source of comfort to you and confirmation of our noble intentions. He told us about your experiences. Trouble with trust. I'll leave you with this, though. Keep an open mind about things. Back in January, no one could have predicted the world we live in today. Even when it started to unravel, we still couldn't accept it. Before meeting them, the others as you called them, I thought I reached my limit of what I could believe," Doc said, then chuckled. "I hadn't even grazed it. Most of the time I still don't believe it. Makes me think I've made this whole thing up. That I fell asleep at the wheel and have been dreaming ever since. Like my relatives are all gathered around, you know. On their cell phones, likely."

Jean stuttered, "I'm sorry I don't–"

Doc draped his hand over hers, "Just keep an open mind is all. Whatever you think might have happened to our loved ones, turned them into Stargazers, the truth is going to be a tough pill to swallow. I had my own thoughts, my own guess. I can't say I'm relieved to be wrong about it. If anything, I'm more confused."

Michael refused to leave Jean's side until his cigarette craving sent him skittering around the room like a spider trapped in a bathroom sink. He smoked outside her window to keep an eye on her. She ate and drank more, spoke further with Doc about the realities of life with one hand, as well as the additional injuries that announced themselves as the fog in her brain cleared. Mostly cuts and bruises, all healing as expected.

Throughout the conversation, Jean slipped into micro-naps that often went unnoticed by Doc, who could seemingly speak for minutes without pausing for breath. That her eyes were hidden behind bandages contributed to the pattern.

"Oh, I think I hear Lucy," Doc said, then left the room.

Jean succumbed to exhaustion in the thirty seconds Doc was absent, head slumped to the side on her pillow.

"Hello there, Jean. I'm Lucy, but Doc prolly told ya that already. Some folks call me Red on account of my hair, but I guess that name don't fit no more since I ain't been to a parlor since before Christmas and my secret's out in the open. God, that feels like a lifetime ago. How are ya?"

Their interaction had the rhythm of old friends catching up after a time apart. Lucy was a decade younger than Jean but cut from a similar cloth. She lived a life that was mostly good, an under-appreciated fact until the world caught fire. It was also tough. Failed marriages to men she referred to by individual slurs as opposed to names. There was *the jackass*, who came before *the asshole*. There was also a *dumb sonofabitch* who might have departed her life more recently.

The hotel job was an effort to get out of the sun after a skin cancer scare in her mid-thirties. Though she spent much of her working life around roughnecks and cowboys, she found the hard work and honesty carried over well. She hated the uniform, though. Said she would rather wear a thong backwards than choke herself with another neck scarf.

"Doc was sorta coy about the others you were with. Had a lot to say about you, but I couldn't get a handle on them. What can you tell me? Am I readin' it wrong?" Jean asked during a lull between stories. Doc was also out of the room preparing dinner.

"Oh, well, I guess that's not so easy to talk about."

"Why? Should I be worried?"

"Yeah, in general. You *should* be worried forever and always, startin' from about two months ago, give or take a week."

"Why can't you ..."

Lucy's hand squeezed her thigh, "Because you'd think I was crazy 'fore I got five minutes in. While you're under our care I can't risk that. You'd dive right through that window the second I turned my back. I know you can't see it, but I'm pointin' just across the room there."

Michael had fallen asleep in an overstuffed chair he hauled to the foot of the bed. His snores served as intermittent white noise for their conversation.

Jean whispered, "Does Michael know? Have you told him?"

Lucy replied in a soft voice, "He knows they're here to help. I'm not sayin' he ain't smart enough to get it, but it's a lot to take in. And it's a burden. If they haven't told him, I s'pose there's a reason for it."

"When will I meet them? I mean, I feel stupid for askin' this, but with all that's happened I guess it's reasonable to assume things. Are they human?"

Lucy sighed, squeezed Jean's thigh again.

"Dinner's ready!" Doc called from the kitchen.

The white noise stopped as Michael roused in his chair and woke smacking his lips.

"They don't come every night. One does most nights. As for your question, keep goin' with that thought. It'd prolly be good for you to start thinkin' of possibilities on your own. Maybe if you think of somethin' wild enough it won't be such a shock to hear the truth."

Jean slept, her belly full of venison and steamed vegetables. She had to stop Lucy from recounting the successful hunt, the bubbly blood trail she followed to the fallen buck. Michael slept beside her, curled into a ball in the overstuffed chair, Gunny to the right of his footrest.

She woke not knowing if it was morning or the middle of the night but guessed the former by the fullness of her bladder. The path to the restroom was easy to navigate after practicing several times before going to bed. During her return, her ears reported Michael was still asleep in his chair, breathing loudly through his mouth. She climbed back into bed but sat up instead of sinking into the pillows.

"Hello?" she whispered, left hand searching the air in front of her.

The voice did not belong to Michael, Doc, or Lucy. It was gentle, and strange, as if an animal she could not picture had been given the power of speech.

"Hello. We are well met. Rest now for as long as you need. For when you wake, we have much to discuss."

APOCALYPSE RADIO

Hello friends, CK here. I'd like to begin with an apology for the previous ... is *episode* the right word? Broadcast? That feels better. I'd like to apologize for the previous broadcast. I get the sense the few of you who do listen ...

(sighs)

That's self-deprecating. There's hundreds of you accordin' to my log. That is, uh, folks who contacted me to let me know they're listenin'. From an idea, a shot in the dark a month or so ago, we're on our way to buildin' that community I've referenced a few times now. I could sense you, some number of you, tunin' out. It was unhinged. Pointless. Most importantly, it was unhelpful.

I promise it won't happen again. I can't promise I won't be wrong about things. I'll probably pass along bad information in the hopes of helpin' to avoid some catastrophe or other. I'll make mistakes. What I won't do is be seduced by the fantastic. Not to say I don't believe in it. I just won't broadcast conjecture, a supposition. Because you need somethin' to hold onto, somethin' that exists outside of a stranger's mind.

According to the calendar, we're about to welcome a new season. A season for life, for growth. 99.8% of humanity did not survive this winter, but we did. Does that make us special? I don't know. What do we have in common? Maybe if we learn the answer to that question we'll know then. A fair number of us .2% won't be here this time next year. That's not me bein' sensationalist. Most of us are surviving on what was left behind. I am. I had no portable greenhouse stocked for the end times. No, I'm eatin' Doritos and Ramen spiked with jerky.

How's your water? Do you have a source other than what you can pilfer from the rapidly dwindlin' shelves? If not, that's priority number one. I imagine if you're hearin' my voice, you've secured a shelter that might not last forever but will do for now. Someday you're gonna have to travel. Maybe against your will. Maybe those dwindlin' shelves will finally run empty. You're gonna realize water is heavy. It takes up space. In a trunk or in a backpack. You need more of it than you might guess, especially if you're on foot.

When you take that plunge and hit the road, you might want to consider more than just the highway system. Yes, the shortest path between two points is a straight line, and the roads are pretty good about bein' mostly straight, but your road might be dry as the squirrel bones in the attic. Look for rivers and lakes, ponds in a pinch. If you're travelin' more than just a handful of miles, you need to figure water into the equation. And that water has to be purified. Do you remember Oregon Trail? Dysentery?

Food is a different story. Eventually, the natural world will sort itself out. Might take years, decades even, to stabilize, to reach a new normal. For the moment, there's an abundance of prey in the form of livestock, and a shortage of predators. That's where you come in. You can't be a pacifist. You need the protein and, there's a finite number of protein bars left in the world. Beyond that, apex predator, it's time to earn your station. I'll think of you when I'm eatin' my jerky Ramen tonight. Think of me when I'm skinnin' a raccoon six months from now, 'cause my jerky done run out, and I just don't have it in me to put a cow down.

I'm no expert on survival. I did print out as much as I could before the net went offline. To be honest, I haven't looked at it.

I will. When I do, I'll share what I learn. Just not in the right state of mind at the moment. Feels like something I'll need to force myself to do, and it's hard to feel the pressure to do it when the eatin's still okay.

More to come on the survival front, but I'd be happy to share any lessons learned out in the field, so to speak.

In elephant watch news, the pachyderms have reversed course and are headed east toward the Texas hill country. Slowly, I'm told. I wonder if they could sense the desert loomin' before 'em. Animals can do that, can't they?

Goddamnit, I just realized I messed the order up again. I'm supposed to put the feel-good shit at the end. Isn't that how you're supposed to deliver bad news? Sandwich it in the middle?

This might be more strange than bad, although I can't say it's good under any definition of the word. And I'll stay in my lane when I tell it. Heard from more than one person, so I think the info is legit.

There's lights in the sky. Not stars, not satellites. Somethin' else, I'm told. They've been seen around those strange structures the Stargazers built. One fella said they reminded him of stories of Will-o'-the-wisps, ghost lights. Now, I might tack a report like that on the end of the broadcast and call it interesting if not good, but there's another story to go with it that is categorically the former and not the latter.

Remember the warnin' about the savages off the interstate over in Kansas? The guys huntin' people for sport? Remember that poor soul they turned into a scarecrow? There was a group passin' through, unaware of the danger. They learned about the radios and my broadcast a few days later. Guess there's folks out there makin' signs about it and postin' them on the highways. Thanks for that.

Anyway, off track. This group said the scarecrow-man was alive. Come up on him in the mornin' and he was flappin' what limbs he could. They rushed over to help and got a better look. He was pretty well chewed up by birds. Had no eyes, jaw hangin' by a thread on one side. No way he was alive despite the flappin' hands. They thought he might have been a Stargazer. Someone corralled it and crucified it. But Stargazers die just like you and me. Seen plenty of dead ones since this all went down.

This thing arches its neck the best it can, and then it belches out one of those ghost lights. The scarecrow went limp, and the light hovered over the group. They said it felt menacing, like a threat. And they ran, this light chasin' 'em down the interstate. Ran until their lungs couldn't take it.

Then it was gone.

(bottle uncorks)

'Scuse me while I tend to my nerves. I can't get past the imagery to give any thought to what happened. Like I said, probably not a good thing.

So, in addition to everything else you need to be afraid of ... add ghost lights to the list.

Chapter Seven

It's the Same Sun Above You

May

The air smelled of growing things, pollen and desert blooms like fireworks trapped in time. It was a good smell when it didn't send Jean into a sneezing fit. Those had become more common in the past two months. She still wore gauze over her eyes, and a side effect of her faltering vision was a fixation on the inputs from the other senses. She hesitated to consider them enhancements. That would put too rosy a stamp on something she did not accept; Doc's hope for her sight was unfounded. That Doc no longer mentioned her eyes was an indication of the direction of his thoughts.

"Trouble?" he said.

His words were imprecise, often missing the mark but close enough to it Jean had no difficulty understanding. It was as if he had an internal thesaurus and sometimes referred to the second page of synonyms rather than the first. *Ted* was the name he offered when Doc introduced them. Ted had introduced himself, in a way, the night after Jean woke in the new house. But he didn't linger, and he didn't offer his name at that time. It didn't fit him. His voice or presence. However, his true name would not make sense to her, he claimed. *Like teeth rattling in a can.*

"Trouble?" she repeated, turning her face his direction.

She wished she could see him. Him and his ilk. Doc described them in great detail, using the same descriptor for Ted's hair, tinsel, she'd thought when glimpsed the day at the baseball fields. Each time she envisioned Ted it was a different face. Her fingertips were not sensitive enough to convert textures into a picture in her brain, and she would never have asked to touch him that way. Doc said his skin was the color of an old penny, and that was easy enough to envisage. It was the structure of his face she could not pin down, could not harvest it from her memory.

"With my words," he clarified.

Jean inhaled and rocked back a few inches, then allowed the chair to carry her forward.

"I think *trouble* is not quite what I'm experiencing. I'm in my fifties, you know? I've got all these years of knowin' what's right about the world, knowin' it as well as I know just how a Dr. Pepper tastes before I take the first sip. I've walked this world for decades. Decades. Now, startin' with what happened in January, I'm like a baby again, and everything I thought I knew was wrong."

Ted frowned, "Not wrong. If you learned the fruit you name *apple* was actually named *malum*, would you have been wrong? Apples are named many words, including *malum*."

"But that's just the difference in language. I mean, I can accept apple has a different name in other languages ..."

"Think further. What in your memories is wrong now? Instead of one story you now have another. Instead of one explanation you now have another. You were not wrong to believe your old stories. Your truth was true up until it wasn't. You are like a fish who believes the whole of the universe is four glass walls, that food falls from the sky. There are no monsters in the sea grass. Now I have given you the ocean, and you feel much smaller within it."

He mouthed words he did not speak, and Jean squealed as something tickled her cheek.

His laugh was like thunder, "Forgive me, friend! I so enjoy your sounds. It was simply a butterfly."

Jean shook her head and brandished her stump. "If I still had this hand, I'd sock you good!"

"Sock?"

"Punch."

"Ah, sock is punch."

Jean smoothed her shirt and sat a little taller in her chair.

"It's not what you said, you know. It's not that I can't accept there's more outside of my glass walls. You kinda got close talkin' about food fallin' from the sky. It's like the fake skull at the bottom of the aquarium. My whole life I knew just how it got there, by whose hand. Now, you're tellin' me that was just a story, one of many."

Jean followed the sound of his movement as he stood and stepped away from the shade of the porch. When describing Ted, Doc remarked how he was almost always shirtless. If it was cold, he wore an animal hide vest but never for long. Jean wondered if Doc was pulling her leg about that last part.

"It's the same sun above you. You breathe the same air. While you question all you know of the universe and your place in it, the universe has not stuttered for one moment to consider you. Not one butterfly moved its migration to research you. The ... aquarium and the ocean can both exist. Your stories and the truth you now know can both exist."

Jean stood and held out her hand. "Help me down to ya, Ted."

He obliged, walking her down the steps to the sidewalk cutting through the garden. She smelled them, then, the fruit of Doc's labor. While cooking, he spoke about the green thumb that coaxed stalks and tender shoots from desert soil that, in the wild, supported a subtler bounty. Gunny could not piss on them fast enough and was unbothered by Lucy's threats to piss in his food bowl in revenge. Jean tilted her face.

"I can feel it. The sun. It feels the same even if I can't see the light."

Ted draped an arm around her shoulders, surprising her again with his height.

"You will see the light Jean. When you are ready."

"If you say so."

"Shall we walk white dog?" he asked. According to Ted, *Gunny* was not the dog's real name, though he did not offer a substitute, instead referring to him as *white dog* as if there were many he might be confused with.

Jean pursed her lips, "That depends. Are you gonna tell me some new story that's gonna ruin my brain?"

He laughed again, vibrating the marrow in Jean's bones.

"I am going to answer one of the first questions you asked me. I am going to tell you about what attacked you and stole your eyes."

Michael returned from a supply run with Lucy just as Jean, Ted, and white dog were setting out.

"I got lots of cigarettes!" Michael said, then shrugged. "They're the girl kind, but they taste the same."

Ted's walks felt directionless to Jean. When she inquired about them, he explained it was the act of moving that would help her understanding.

"Your mind is less likely to harden, to build barriers when it is concentrating on the next step."

Jean challenged his assertion, as she did with his myriad proclamations about everything from the optimal time of the day to move one's bowels to the superiority of a two-nap system to sleeping through the night. He was right about the walking, and Jean's bowel movements were now so predictable even Gunny memorized them and would walk to the bathroom door moments before she approached it. She had not adopted the two-nap system, though suspected Ted was also right about that.

Doc insisted Jean use a cane to aid her navigation, and she refused, opting for a walking stick he had previously used for hiking. Ted never led her into any obstacles, and so the stick was mostly employed to tap Michael's heels when he began to lag.

"Let us return to the apple," Ted began.

Michael led the group, tossing a tennis ball up the path Gunny sometimes retrieved.

"Let us," Jean replied.

"I want you to grow your understanding of life," Ted said. As he paused, Jean wondered if *grow* was a word she should substitute in her mind. "You would name the color of the apple *red*. You would also name the color of winter gift man *red*."

Jean had been sipping from her water bottle at the mention of *winter gift man* and spat a mouthful on the dirt.

"Winter gift man?" she said.

"You cannot see it, but I am smoothing my belly," Ted said.

"Santa Claus."

"Right. Winter gift man is Santa Claus. You would name his suit red, and you would name the apple red. These are not the same color if you put them together. But they are both red. Therefore, there are many colors you would name red."

"A spectrum?" Jean offered.

Ted slowed his pace, "Hmm. Yes, I think that is the right name. Spec-trum. Such is the same with life. Life is a beating heart, skin and blood. Life is also roots and leaves. And it is so much more. Smaller than you can see, older than you could imagine."

"Older than me?" Jean said.

Ted's laugh sounded like a punch to the gut, a sort of cough/bark hybrid.

"How old do you believe *me* to be?"

Jean pointed to her left, "Older than that mountain?"

"How did you know there was a mountain?" Ted asked, then barked laughter. "There are mountains all around us! Possible. I have not spoken to that mountain to know its age, and mountains are not good at remembering things like that. I am walking off the tracks, Jean. But I accuse you for being so funny.

"There are things that are alive, things that have died and become something else, and things that have never lived. What attacked you was something that has never lived."

"How do you know?"

They caught up to Michael, grumbling about unsuccessfully attempting to light his cigarette. As if trapped in the core of a tornado, the wind assaulted him on all sides, Jean imagined by the sound of his shirt flapping.

"Cup your hands around it," Jean suggested.

"I tried!"

"Well, maybe it's time to give it up then."

"Hi Ted!" Michael said, his frustration momentarily subdued. "Can you do the thing?"

"Describe it for me," Jean said.

"Michael is giving me the white stick, and I am placing it in his mouth."

"Okay," Jean said.

"Think about fire. Really think about it. Make a picture in your head. Michael's eyes are closing now. He is showing his teeth like white dog. He is really trying. Can you see it?" Ted asked.

"I can see it!"

SNAP

"Wow!" Michael said out of the corner of his mouth.

"You are just as joyful as the first time! Let us continue."

Jean followed the crunch of desert dirt beneath Michael's shoes and the scent of burning tobacco. Though her elbow was hooked inside Ted's, he did not pull.

"White dog is in front of you. He is like a lost little cloud. His limbs are like a baby deer. Can you sense him out there?"

Jean pivoted her head like a satellite looking for a lost signal. She thought she felt him to the left, like a little tug on her soul from that direction.

"Your eyes can be troublesome because they make your heart forget the truth of what it knows," Ted said.

"Ah, so bein' blind is a good thing?"

"I do not like that word."

"Blind?"

"No. Good. The universe does not wonder about such things. A rock is not good or bad but can be used for what you would call good or bad. What you could see, when you had eyes, is small beside all there is to know."

"C'mon Gunny!" Michael called, and by the sound of it he was speaking around a cigarette.

"I am sorry, Jean. I was bothered by white dog chasing his tail. What was I saying?" Ted said.

Jean smiled at the word *bothered* and replied, "Before you tried to convince me bein' blind wasn't good or bad, you were gonna tell me how you know the thing that attacked the car was something that never lived."

"Right. I know this because there is no other possibility that I can see."

Jean scoffed, "You know it's true because you know that it's true?"

"Exactly!" Ted said, then furrowed his brows. "Oh, that was a rude joke."

"Sarcasm."

"Hmm. We are not good at understanding it."

"Gods don't understand sarcasm?"

"Do *you* understand the language of mountains?"

Jean said, "I ain't gonna say no because I haven't tried. Could be I'm fluent in it. You're walkin' off the tracks again, Ted."

"Right. There is much you cannot see, but you know it is there. You cannot see oxygen but never question your lungs are filled with it. Your friends, Henry and Nickel–"

"Penny."

"Right. Henry and Penny are alive. You know this, but you do not *know* it as you know the taste of Mr. Pepper before you drink it. Where do you know it?"

Jean stopped, leaned on her walking stick and turned her face to the sun again. At times she felt she could see the world around her, could sense the mountains and the mesquite, the shrubs and cacti. It was the same sense of waking up and knowing Michael was sleeping in the overstuffed chair, even on the rare occasions he was not snoring. She did not have to see him to know he was there. When she thought of Misfit her heart was full, not fearful. When she thought of Marcus it was like a specter's hand unfurling in her chest.

Henry and Penny ... heart full.

There was a little less definition when she recalled their faces. She remembered Penny's dimples but might have forgotten the precise shape of her ears, the direction Henry parted his hair. The softening of her memory had no influence over the confidence of her heart. That's where she felt it. If not in the organ directly then right around it.

"Here," Jean said patting her sternum.

"And what does it feel like there?"

Ted's hand pressed the small of her back.

"Yes, yes. Walk so I do not build barriers," Jean said.

She shuffled along, walking stick tapping the ground but not deliberately. The smell of cigarette smoke intensified, meaning Michael managed to light one on his own.

"It feels like when you're walkin' down the stairs and you forget how many stairs there are. You expect a certain distance, but it ends up bein' shorter, to the floor you know? That little jolt inside. It's like that but contained. If that feeling was a ball inside my chest. That's what it feels like."

"You cannot see it, but I am small clapping for you."

"You cannot see it, but I am flippin' you off with my right hand," Jean replied.

Ted laughed, "The long finger! That is funny because your hand is gone."

"Careful, or I'll use my good hand."

"We are walking off the tracks together. And I don't want to conquer you with too much information. I can sense that which is alive, that which has died and become something else, and that which has never lived. It is as simple as smelling Michael's cigarettes or seeing the green ball in white dog's mouth."

"Good for you."

"Yes, it is. And it started like you described. Many years ago. Thousands? I do not know. I was not in this form."

Jean stopped again, "Wait. So, you can sense the things that haven't lived. Okay, got it. I'll ask more about that later. You can sense that which is alive. Can you sense them? Henry and Penny?"

"Certainly. I sensed all of you before we met–"

"Where are they?! Why haven't you taken me to them?" Jean said, brandishing her walking stick.

Ted placed one hand atop hers.

"We are in a new world, now. Hold onto your stories, and know it is the same sun above you. But also know you have a responsibility in this new world, to Henry and Nickel. For this responsibility, you are on the right tracks. We are keeping them safe. And it will not be long."

"Keepin' them safe …" Jean trailed off. "Ted. Could you have stopped it from happening? The thing that attacked me?"

Ted pressed the small of her back again, ushering her forward.

"If I had been with you, yes."

"But you wouldn't have. Because this was supposed to happen."

"Something like that."

They walked in silence for a time. Jean tried to concentrate on the feeling in her chest, what she imagined as a ball of nervous energy. A few minutes later, they caught up to Michael sitting on a boulder, Gunny asleep and snoring in the shade of it.

"Are we done?" Michael asked, his undefined words indicating an unlit cigarette bobbed on his bottom lip.

"We can be," Jean said.

They turned there, Michael lagging and Gunny refusing to leave the shade until the indignity of being left behind sent him galloping to the head of the group.

"I can feel your questions like a storm inside of you. Ask them."

She had many, each seeming more important than the last.

Where did Ted and the others come from?

Why did they come here?

There was no end to the questions in her mind, and she felt little control over the one that eventually passed through her lips.

"Were you always a god?"

Ted laughed, "Remember, Jean, you named us that. We didn't name ourselves."

Apocalypse Radio

No elephant news, but stayin' in what used to be Texas, we now have tigers to deal with. Mailbox off I-35 there was a message, a warnin' more accurately, about tigers claimin' territory all over the piney woods. Suppose it's likely these and other escaped or *liberated* predators encountered Stargazers back when those were a thing. Probably never have an easier time huntin' than when your prey is dumber than a rubber hammer. No offense to the Stargazers. I hope my mom was eaten by somethin' cool, you know? A hyena, maybe.

Suffice it to say, the predators have probably tasted man-flesh before. So, if you see a kitty in your travels, forget that rhyme you learned as a kid 'cause it won't just holler.

Keepin' with the theme, animals are pretty much all I hear about. Animals and the lights. It's been a couple of months since the first report. Where was that from, Kentucky? I think it came in right after the human scarecrow encounter over in Kansas. Thought that might've been a one-off, maybe unrelated to the Stargazers phenomenon. Pile another scoop of bad luck on top of a steamin' pile. As if the Stargazers weren't enough. That's not easy to accept now. 'Cause of the lights.

Dead animals coming back to life, a sort of life anyway. It's no stranger than Grandma takin' a sledgehammer to a skyscraper. At least they got lights in their eyes so you can see 'em at a distance.

We need more information, folks. What have you seen out there? I get the sense it's like ... it's like a ghost puttin' on a costume. Does that sound close to the mark? I don't think the ultimate goal is to become a fallin' apart deer. Based on the stories you've shared with me, the messages left in mailboxes around the country, the goal is for you and me to be the costume.

What happens when they succeed? Have they already and we just don't know about it? I hope not. I've no idea where this piece fits in the puzzle, if it even belongs. But I can't say I heard of anything like it prior to the Stargazers.

If you meet a person with light leakin' around the eyes, be sure to tell me about it, after you run a hundred miles in the other direction.

I think our survey of the monuments is complete, but I can't be sure there aren't some duplicate reports. I'm gonna make a trip in the next couple weeks, see if it's true what they say about 'em. They're hard to look at, makes you sick apparently. Remember that fella that radioed in back in May? Said his mind couldn't make sense of it, that it was so ... unfamiliar it was like his brain malfunctioned. More lights around 'em as well, so I'll be lookin' from a distance.

I wouldn't leave if I didn't have to, but my stores are low. Gonna meet a few radio friends while I'm out. Might do some tradin' as the potato farm was a success, but I can't stand to look at 'em anymore. I'd kill for a salad.

You know, there'll come a time when I won't know what day it is anymore. I would've lost track if not for the calendar in this cabin. I don't imagine calendars will be high on the priority list for whatever society climbs out of this rubble five or fifty years from now. Strange how a day can feel like any other when you don't assign a name to it. I forgot my own birthday. Forgot my mom's birthday.

If you got anything worth throwin' on a grill, today would be a good day for it. Happy Fourth of July, folks. Whatever the fuck that even means now.

Chapter Eight

What Happened? Where Were You?

Henry returned to the window throughout the night, tiptoeing around the squeaky spots in the floorboards so as not to wake Penny. Tamping the flames of her excitement was difficult, and his efforts failed until she fell asleep of her own accord mid-sentence. It was not fear he felt, nor curiosity. Since he fled the motel leaving Jean and Judith behind, life somehow shaped itself into something he would call *normal*. Normal for the times, not in general.

The lights were gone, though the sky was full of stars. Henry understood his *normal* was about to pivot again. The lights were not incidental. They meant something.

"They're so pretty!" Penny had said, waving at the orbs as if they might understand the gesture.

"Yes, they are," Henry murmured with no enthusiasm, hoisting her off the grass and onto his hip.

"Who are they?" she asked.

"You mean *what* are they?" Henry corrected, but he had no answer to either question.

In his previous life, in an environment not dissimilar from that one, he stared at the same night sky and felt equally rudderless, his destination dictated by forces greater than himself. There were so many moments his head did not know the next action to take even as his hands performed them. He became half a dozen men in one, compartmentalizing a screaming man's request to tell his son he died fighting for freedom, as Henry pinched his gushing artery with bare fingers. Was it Henry at the levers? Forcing combat gauze into a wound the size of a small melon? Was it some other part of him he did not fully understand?

There was no one to scream at him, now. He had no training to fall back on. No arteries to pinch. All he could do was wait and hope the pivot might be toward good.

Misfit looked like a pair of mismatched socks on the bed, one dark and one light. Her tail quivered at the sight of him, threatening to thump Penny's sleeping head. Henry danced over the floorboards again, one finger bisecting his lips as Misfit's quiver intensified into a wag. He scooped her off the comforter and tucked her into the crook of his arm.

The sun would rise soon, and Henry knew sleep would not be possible before it did. Rather than lay in bed worrying over what he could not control, he put his restless hands to work. He stocked Ol' Reliable for an emergency evacuation should the need arise. But it didn't have everything required to last beyond a couple of weeks. If the lights were a harbinger of bad things to come, they would head to the northwest.

"There are so many fish you can just pluck 'em out of the river. Don't even need a net," Henry told Penny of their possible future home.

"What about bears?" Penny asked, looking off to the side as if recalling one the nature documentaries she preferred.

"We'll have Misfit!" Henry said.

"Daddy," Penny said, rolling her lips into a thin line. It was the same face Judith made when she concentrated, sometimes on a recipe, often on not telling Henry the truth straining the stitches of her reassembled heart.

"Or we can fish from Ol' Reliable. We'll just stick our poles out the window."

Penny rolled her eyes but later submitted to the logic when her father demonstrated how it was possible. Henry doubted Ol' Reliable would make it that far, but there would be plenty of options along the way. Between the outskirts of Marfa, Texas and some nebulous destination where salmon dreamed of becoming dinner, there were limitless tribulations.

Henry stood on the porch, Misfit writhing to be set free. The sky to the east was a shade lighter than black, but dawn was an hour away.

"Go on. Do your thing," Henry said, and Misfit obliged, rocketing off the porch steps and vanishing in the dark.

His only purpose now was to shield Penny from the horrors beyond their home. It was a finish line he would never cross. Life was simpler in that way. It was also a burden, heavier than any he previously shouldered. One wrong turn, wrong guess could be a death sentence. Henry recalled the voice of the man at the motel, demanding he hand over his daughter to him. Implying what would happen to her when he did. A death sentence might be a blessing.

Part of him, not a small part, wanted to leave then. Before he learned the meaning of the lights. Delaying felt like an invitation. In the past few months, Henry reacquainted himself with firearms. But what would he do against lights in the sky? Shoot them?

Misfit returned, headbutting his calf until he scooped her into his arms.

"What do you think they are? Ghosts?" Henry asked.

She licked his face.

"Yeah, probably not," he said, then walked her back inside. "What do you think of salmon?"

***

"Why we doin' this, Daddy? It's hot out," Penny whined.

"It's hot every day, sweetie. But we're doing it today because it's her birthday," Henry said.

"I don't remember what she looked like."

"Well, you see her when you look in the mirror. Your eyes. Your cheeks. She's there. I'll charge my phone. Eventually. I'll show you pictures of her."

Penny was too out of breath to offer further complaints as she scaled the hill. Her arm went limp, forcing Henry to pull her. This actually made the climb easier, as her weight offset that of the stone pressed against his body on the opposite side. She wasn't interested in the *memorial*, didn't understand what the word meant despite her father explaining it to her multiple times. She wanted to talk about the lights. She wanted it to be night again so she could wait for them. Her daddy didn't see them the same way she did. He didn't understand.

"Isn't it pretty up here?" Henry asked, relinquishing Penny's hand.

Her eyebrows morphed into hump-backed caterpillars. Butterflies were pretty. She perched her hands on her hips and turned in slow circles, thinking she must have missed something for her father to describe the view as *pretty*.

He had that hopeful smile of his, the one that sometimes masked other emotions churning below the surface. Penny spied a cluster of cactuses with fuchsia bulbs that reminded her of Jolly Ranchers. The color was pretty if nothing else was.

"Yeah Daddy," she said.

Henry placed the stone on the ground and propped it up with rocks. He stood, arms crossed over his chest and tapped it with the toe of his boot. The stone tipped, the rocks beneath it scattering.

"That won't do," he said, then kneeled and began to carve a trench in the ground.

Penny sighed and sat in the dirt.

"Daddy, we have to stay up late tonight."

"Why's that?"

"The lights! We have to stay up for the lights!"

"Did they tell you that?"

Penny flicked a pebble, "I don't think they can talk."

"Oh yeah?"

"Well, maybe they can. But they don't got mouths. Maybe they can talk like in your head."

"Oh, so they're psychic lights?" Henry said.

Penny did not understand the word *psychic* but knew by the way her daddy said it he was not serious.

"They're special," Penny said, hoping that would encompass the unfamiliar term. Misfit skittered up the path, providing a timely interruption. "There you are! You been sleepin' all day!"

Penny carried Misfit like a football, pointing at the landmarks visible from the summit of the small hill. Meanwhile, Henry wedged the stone into the trench and bracketed it with rocks. Despite Penny's apparent disinterest, she had spent most of the morning painting flowers around the words Henry had written.

"Okay, sweetie," Henry said and dusted his hands off.

Penny stood beside her father, brows furrowed at the stone.

"What? Something wrong?"

Penny shrugged, kicked a puff of dirt, "It's just that Mommy isn't here."

"I know that sweetie. This is just something for us. When someone *passes* and you don't have a service, a funeral ..." he trailed off. "If there isn't a place you can go to grieve, to feel sad I mean, it can feel like everywhere is that place. This is a place we can go to and think about Mommy. Tell her we miss her. I'll add to it. Put a bench up here. We can bring flowers. Have a picnic."

Penny shrugged.

"It's not just that. The last time you saw Mom was, well, you were there. You know I saw some bad stuff before, right?"

Penny nodded.

"I lost some friends. Not in the way we lost Mom, but it wasn't pretty to see. And as bad as it was then, it was worse later. It got so I couldn't remember anything from before. That last moment, their *worst* moment, was bigger than anything before it. I don't want that for you."

Penny placed Misfit on the ground and faced her father. She extended an arm, jumped and stamped Henry in the chest with an open palm.

"She's in there, Daddy. Remember I told you? She's in there with you and in here with me," Penny said, patting her own chest.

"Yes, but–"

"You don't have to walk up a hill to talk to Mommy. I do it all the time."

Henry scratched a patch of beard on his cheek, "You said you didn't remember what she looked like. I didn't think ..."

Penny's gaze drifted downward and to the side, "I sorta remember. I just don't wanna make you sad talkin' about her."

Henry kneeled, grasped his daughter's chin. "Hey, sweetie, you don't ever have to worry about that. It doesn't make me sad to think about her. Well, I guess it does, but sad in a way I need sometimes. It's how we know this was all real, right? Your mommy and I had a whole life together. If I didn't feel sad about her ..."

Henry's words slowed to a trickle and stopped. Penny caught the steel in his gaze and turned around hoping it was the elephants again. It wasn't, and for a few seconds she did not understand what captured his attention. Then she saw. Two figures walking along the dirt path to their home. Since they fled the motel what felt like half a lifetime ago, there were only fleeting encounters with other people. A few times while out collecting supplies they heard an engine, possibly miles away. When this happened, Henry abandoned the errand and immediately returned home. There was also evidence of others foraging from the same shrinking supply of food in the few remaining convenience stores.

Penny did not enjoy the supply runs. Her daddy's eyes went wide like there were ghosts outside the windows, and he seemed surprised by her presence when she spoke. It reminded her of before, how a scene in a movie could strip the kindness from his face. How his knee bounced outside of his control as he twisted his hands into knots. When that happened, she would grab his cheek and force him to look at her, but she couldn't do that from the backseat.

"Let's go."

Henry yanked her off the ground and wrapped her in a bear hug. After a few paces she could no longer see the figures beyond the hilltop.

"Maybe they're nice people like us," Penny offered.

Henry grunted in response. She felt the tension in his body, muscles taut and hard, shaking as if they might explode out of his skin. The hill's decline propelled him across the lawn, grass as brittle as spider legs crunching underfoot. Misfit raced ahead, scaling the porch steps in one leap. She spun in circles on the welcome mat, delighted by the sudden flurry of activity.

"Go to your hiding place, okay?" Henry said, depositing Penny on the porch.

"What about Misfit?"

Henry shook his head, "She makes too much noise. I'll put her in the truck in case we need to leave in a hurry. You be ready to go too."

"But Daddy–"

"Just go!" he shouted, then closed his eyes and gritted his teeth. "Sweetie, we don't have time to talk about it. Just like we practiced, remember? What are the safe words?"

"*Pickle* means it's safe. *Potato* means I go to the truck."

"You *run* to it. And if you don't hear anything?"

"Stay where I'm at."

Henry dragged his arm across his eyes. It felt like an hour had passed, but it was likely less than five minutes. The topography obscured his view of the road, but he wouldn't leave the porch for a better angle, wouldn't put more distance between himself and Penny than was necessary. He alternated between the rifle's scope and the binoculars he found resting on a book of west Texas birds in the living room. If the intruders followed the road all the way to the house, he should see them at about a quarter mile distance.

Henry dried his hand off on his jeans, then blew on the trigger until the sweat evaporated. In a previous life, in which he understood only one definition of the word *stargazer*, he grew accustomed to waiting and knowing death might be marching toward him. The feeling never left him despite the years and milestones between those days and his new life. If he had no choice, he would do what was necessary. Just like he did to the man at the motel.

What if he did have a choice?

Could he kill someone for the simple mistake of thinking the house was unoccupied?

He had considered erecting threatening signs and posting them along the path to the house but thought it might target them more than serve as a deterrent. As normal as their lives had become, he knew a day like this was inevitable.

"Come on. Come on. Where the fuck are you?" he whispered and returned to the scope.

Maybe they'd spotted him on top of the hill. That was a stupid idea. He could have put the memorial beside the house or under the oak tree Penny liked to climb on. The hill was too exposed. Each time he visited it, he would risk someone seeing them from a distance.

Henry's finger released the trigger, and he retreated from the scope a few inches. He blinked as if staring at the sun, then grabbed the binoculars.

"Is that a fucking wolf?" he said.

For the moment, he was not paying attention to the two figures, blurry behind a wall of shimmering heat. The animal was the size of a juvenile polar bear. It trotted in front of the figures, head raised and scanning the terrain.

Of the possibilities Henry mentally prepared himself for, an attack wolf was not among them. He swapped the binoculars for the scope again. The beast's head was the size of a cannon-ball. The ears were limp, though. Didn't wolves have pointy ears? Henry swallowed and refocused on the people a few paces behind.

A man and a woman, he determined. The man had stopped and was attempting to light a cigarette pinched between his teeth with the stub of another. He was tall and lanky, all knees and elbows. The woman to his right wore sunglasses that ob-scured half her face. She leaned on a walking stick and seemed to be smiling.

"What the f–" he began. She was smiling at him. As if she could see him. He was hidden behind an old trunk he'd lugged downstairs just for this purpose. She couldn't see him from that far away. He'd be a blur if anything. It *felt* like she was smiling at him, though.

There was a dead mesquite on the right side of the path to the house. In its blackened branches was a single red Christmas ornament. For this scenario, intruders walking up to the house, the ornament indicated the threshold beyond which Henry's shot would be accurate from the porch. The beast, a giant dog he decided, had already passed it. The man and woman did a few seconds later. The man had successfully transferred the fire from one cigarette to another and seemed delighted with the achievement.

Henry licked his lips. It was so damn dry here. It seemed like the only time he wasn't thirsty was when he was drinking water. There was something tucked under the woman's arm. Green and reflective. It flashed when it caught the sun.

Henry pulled his finger off the trigger and glared at the rifle, wondering how close he'd come. He stood and should have been visible to the approaching figures.

For six months, outside of fleeting encounters, always at a distance, Henry was unaware of another soul. He began to wonder if the items missing from store shelves, the far-off purr of a car engine, was in his mind. What if he and Penny were the last people on Earth? How would they know?

It was the sour cream and onion chips that filled the gap in his understanding. He descended the steps and stood on the broken grass. He wanted to run to her, but between them was a tank of a dog who just then noticed him. The man began to wave, and Henry returned the gesture. He saw her lips move, heard her faint words.

"It's okay, boy. It's okay. He's a friend."

Whether he understood the words or the tone, the dog's posture relaxed. Henry walked forward, squinting. There was something off about her free hand, the one not holding the walking stick.

"Oh no," Henry said, the strange dimensions of her anatomy making sense as they neared. Her hand was missing.

The dog reached him first, and its size was no less impressive up close. It stood on its hind legs and planted two massive paws on either shoulder. Its black marble eyes locked onto Henry's, panting, showing a mouthful of teeth.

"Gunny! Leave him be!" she said, walking faster now, the rocks and debris in her path never underfoot.

The young, smoking man extended his hand, which Henry took.

"I'm Michael" he said, in a voice a couple of octaves higher than Henry would have predicted.

"Henry."

"These are probably all broken, but I thought y'all would appreciate the gesture," Jean said, offering the green bag.

"Jean …" Henry began. There were so many ways to die between the motel and that house in the desert. The days since ached from one end to the other. He believed their parting was a sacrifice, if not to Judith directly then to any number of horrors after.

"I told you I'd find you. Didn't think it'd take this long, and that I'd lose a hand and my eyes in the process. But here I am."

Henry took the chips and pulled her into an embrace, his chin quivering beside her temple. He was not alone. *They* were not alone. There was a possible future in which Henry and Penny never heard another human voice. It was a world he would leave before her, and the silence he left behind was worse than any fate he could imagine.

"What happened? Where were you?" Henry said, taking a step back to appraise her again.

"Oh, just a little car accident. It's a long story, but it ain't the longest story you're gonna hear. I met this one," Jean said, nodding toward Michael. "And the polar bear early on. Might've found my way to you a lot sooner if they were the only ones I met. After the accident, though, I met some more folks. And, Henry, whatever you think happened back in January, I got some whoppers for ya."

Henry shook his head. "I don't understand."

Jean cackled. "That makes two of us! But not understandin' it and not believin' it are two different things. The understandin' will come. You'll meet them. In fact, I think you already have."

As she spoke, her head drifted to the side. She appeared to look in the direction of the house. Hadn't she said something about losing her eyes? Maybe that was an exaggeration.

"Daddy," Penny said in a flat, annoyed voice. "You forgot to say pickle."

Apocalypse Radio

Good day, friends. You may recognize my voice, as I occasionally share these airwaves with our mutual friend. Apocalypse Radio. Hmmm. What would be on your playlist? Instinct pulls me toward melancholy, but perhaps uplifting would be more suitable. What if you wake up in purgatory and the soundtrack to your forever is the last song you heard in life?

Come to think of it, I might prefer a sad song in that case. I don't know if I could tolerate a happy song for eternity. It would feel like God laughing at you.

I'm Maurice. That was my name in the before times and it is today. CK invited me to host in his absence. Don't know if the broadcast will travel as far, considering my orientation to the relays, but I digress. CK is meeting up with fellow survivors to survey a monument. I begged him not to go. It's a dangerous world out there, and the monuments might be the worst part. I saw one in the early days, not too long after the cities fell. I did not - could not look at it directly. Some survivors suggest it's like staring at the sun, and I would argue the opposite. The sun is light and life. This is what comes after the light is gone, when the only evidence of life is just radio waves chasing each other toward the edge of the Universe, voices of men so long dead they might as well have never lived.

I will not abuse the privilege of this invitation stoking fear. We have enough to be afraid of. However, I will share what I communicated to CK in my futile attempt to redirect his energies. We have taken to calling them monuments, maybe for lack of a more suitable term. In unprecedented times there may not be a more suitable term. Imagine you discover a new color. You could only ever describe it by comparing it to known colors. Do you see? Monument may not be the appropriate term, but it's the closest to the mark.

What is the purpose of a monument? To be seen. By whom? Well, those closest to them will be the first to know.

Let us put that one on the shelf for the moment. I will honor the time I have been afforded by offering a *state of the aftermath*. Think of it as the state of the union for our times. The mystery is of secondary concern, because it does not, for now, influence our reality. Our reality is the thousands of us still walking this strange land. You may not check your calendar as often, if at all, but there are months that end in -ber coming, and many of us will be saying as much then. A good number of us did not survive the winter.

Just ... something to think about.

As I was. Back to the state of the aftermath. Word has spread and there are now hundreds, possibly more than a thousand survivors listening and communicating amongst yourselves. The mailboxes are also being used. Sharing information and insight just as CK envisioned. Unless we relearn how to make batteries, we may not have radios in ten years. We will need a new platform, a Pony Express for our era. Alternatively, we can crawl out of our caves and bomb shelters and organize, reform our communities even if we keep a polite distance.

It's something CK and I disagree on. He believes greater numbers means a more appealing target. Why go after a hornet when you can eliminate the hive? CK compared it to bowling if memory serves. The closer the pins, the easier it is to fall them with a single attempt.

Logical, yes. However, CK had no answer for the query I posited. Who, or what, is hurling the bowling ball? Not the Stargazers. There are none left. Not enough meat on the yellowing bones to reanimate. The animals? Yes, the idea of a raccoon with glowing eyes is terrifying, but it is not a harbinger of our second demise. Yes, congregating is risky, but not because some faceless cosmic bowler will topple our tightly clustered souls more easily. We are alive on accident, on purpose, or something in between. Whatever our destiny, we are likely powerless to alter it.

I believe our distance is more of a threat. Bad water or no water. Exposure. Death comes for us all. If you are alone, you will meet him alone.

There are small communities already. In Minnesota, in Arkansas. Probably others we do not have contact with. We are not rebuilding. I think we are waiting to learn if it is worth it. Is it over? Are they–is *it* done with us? It was barely two seasons ago our brothers and sisters left us. But outside my window, it's beginning to feel like they were never here. The road is crisscrossed with green rivers. The homes too far from a population center to matter look like corpses. The shingles like old skin waiting for a rain to slough off.

The state of our aftermath is broken. We are like rats each clinging to our own sliver of a sinking ship. Wildfires become infernos. Hurricanes arrive on our shores unnamed and unplanned-for. The weather should be the worst of it, but mankind always finds a way to maximize despair. Rapists and murderers have established their own little kingdoms. Some have even used our mailbox system against us, luring travelers down unsafe paths.

All of this would be enough, but it isn't. Perhaps the Stargazers were the lucky ones. There is the matter of the lights. We do not know why or how, only what they do. The lights resurrect the dead. Animal or human. These *creatures* are restless. They are not content in brittle forms. They wander from one to another, granting the body an echo of its former life before passing onto the next. Always, they search for us. I have experienced it.

I saw the light from a distance, twin glints a few shades darker than amber. It was in the body of a fawn. And it saw me. Not with the eyes. There were no eyes, only holes. It saw me and ran. The flesh and bones were too weak and, like a boulder breaking apart tumbling down a mountain, the animal came undone. A hind leg was left behind, then another. It ran on its front legs and exited the body once it was near enough.

(sighs)

Hmmm. I suppose if I ever have the time for it, I will adopt a second career. We will need new words moving forward. Words to describe something that has never previously occurred. There is no fair comparison to the sensation of the light, the orb desperate to … enter my person. It felt like a magnet attempting to liberate my heart from my chest. Like, like I don't know.

My words fail me once again, but I have all the time in the world to create new ones. Maurice's Revised American Dictionary. Keep an eye out.

I was not conscious of the battle. My mind was not engaged. But, there was a war going on. The essential *it* versus the essential *I*.

I must have won. The light is gone, and I am still here.

(clears throat)

The state of the aftermath is broken. Our tomorrow does not have to be. If we come together, not in spirit but in reality.

I may still have the reins for the next edition of Apocalypse Radio. I am not a praying man, but I will be thinking of CK tonight. I hope he finds what he is looking for and returns to us safe on the other side of it.

It has been my pleasure sharing the airwaves with you. I leave with a parting suggestion.

Do not let them in.

Chapter Nine

It is Not the First Time We Have Met

After more hugs, half-attempts at filling the gaps of the previous six months, the sun drove the group indoors. Penny seemed intent on using all the words she had not spoken since they'd separated. She brought Jean items of interest collected during supply runs and walks around the property. Each time she returned with something new she appeared surprised at Jean's blindness. She would place the item on the dining room table and lead Jean's good hand to it.

"This is a real shiny rock. Well, it's not shiny like alumi-al ... alumin ... *tin* foil. It's got little bits of shiny in it. You know?"

Michael explored the home, which functioned as an eco-tourist resort in its former life.

"There's so many rooms!" he called from somewhere on the second level.

"More than enough for the two of you," Henry said, patting Jean's hand. "What about the others? Can't beat this set up. Cool water from the well. Fruit trees and plenty of canned goods in the basement. Wine too."

"Oh yeah?" Jean said.

"I can't tell you if it's any good. Haven't dabbled as I always want to have my wits about me. Last thing I need is a repeat of the psycho at the motel while I'm drunk off wine."

"Well, I'm here now. I can take a turn."

"Shoot well with no eyes?" Henry asked, hoping the smile was evident in his voice.

"No. I just shoot a lot. Only need one to hit, right? As for the others, they should be along shortly. Some at least."

Henry reached across the table to squeeze her shoulder.

"I missed you, Jean. We only knew each other for, what, three or four days? Something like that?"

"Somethin' like that."

"It was enough. I knew you were a good person the minute we met."

"If I recall, I was sittin' in a pool of blood."

"You were next to it. And you were kind enough not to kill me."

"Well, I felt the same Henry. I knew you and your little one were good people. Strange, though, isn't it? How you could know that about a person."

Footsteps rumbled down the stairs. Before another interruption could happen, Henry took Jean's hand again, "Some things you just know."

Jean nodded slowly, her thoughts drifting away from the dining room table. She had taken many walks with Ted, had brief interactions with his ilk, who were usually on some errand he would not explain. It was easier to accept the idea there were things she *just knew* after those talks. Each time, it seemed, he grasped a thread of her understanding of a topic, time or love or something similarly abstract, and yanked it. By the end, she was left with a pile of string she did not recognize. In place of these unraveled truths was simple knowing, stripped of its grime or padding.

"We forgot Misfit!" Penny hollered as she dashed through the dining room.

In seconds there was a screech of hinges.

"My goodness, we did forget about her!" Jean said, standing up. "We'll have to introduce her to Gunny."

Henry took her by the elbow and led her to the front door.

"Not afraid he'll eat her, are you?"

"Oh, heavens no. He may look like a polar bear, but he's soft as a lamb. You wouldn't know it to hear him bark, though! My, can that dog make a racket!"

Misfit's paws thrashed as if ground lay beneath her, not air.

"Hold on, Misfit. Just hold on," Penny said.

Gunny sat with his hind legs to the side, head tilted and sinking into his neck as he considered the writhing bundle in Penny's arms. Misfit exploded free, legs a blur as she somersault-ed.

"I said hold on!" Penny whined, giving chase.

Misfit took off trailing a horizontal smokestack of dust and debris. She disappeared around the side of the house and was pursued by Penny, who was determined to introduce the dogs properly.

"I think Misfit-" Henry began and paused tracking the sound of movement around the back of the house.

Within fifteen seconds Misfit was back, tiny legs bucking as she twirled in circles before Gunny. The white dog blinked, head sinking further into his torso. He looked from Jean to Henry and back to the miniaturized bronco. His massive, white paw lifted into the air and hung there, its shadow striping Misfit's back.

"Oh!" Henry said.

"What?" Jean asked.

"He smushed her!" Penny cried.

She crouched before him and grunted, tugging the paw as Misfit wriggled free.

"That's called the *pyr paw* according to Doc. He says Gunny is a Great Pyrenees, and they're known for doin' it. I've got enough scratches on my thighs to attest to it. It's harmless. Just annoying as hell."

Misfit's black mask wormed between Gunny's paws, and she spun to face him. As if just realizing he'd been sitting on a fire ant hill, Gunny jolted to life. His hindquarters aimed at the sky, tail hanging like a question mark.

"Oh, he looks like he wants to play," Henry said.

"That's good, Gunny. This is Misfit. She's part cat but she doesn't use a litter box," Penny said.

Gunny swatted Misfit with his *pyr paw* then rocketed away. Misfit righted herself and gave chase with an ecstatic Penny following close behind.

"They're friends!" Penny squealed and disappeared around the side of the house.

Henry took Jean's arm again, "That went pretty well. Let's get out of this sun and I'll get you a drink. The well water isn't ice cold, but it's damn close."

"That sounds like heaven," Jean said.

* * *

Doc and Lucy arrived mid-afternoon, the former with a basketful of vegetables harvested from his garden.

"You didn't tell me he was so handsome," Lucy said as she shook Henry's hand.

"I honestly kinda forgot what he looked like," Jean said.

"Are those peach trees?" Doc asked as he handed off the produce.

"Yeah, they're ..." Henry began but found himself talking to the back of Doc's head.

"He's big on gardening," Lucy said, one hand bracketing her mouth as if passing gossip.

"Picked the best profession and pastime for the end times if you ask me," Jean said. "A healer and a grower."

"It's like cheating in Oregon Trail. You ever play that?" Lucy said with a wink.

Henry smiled. "Yep. I always picked the banker, and it always came back to bite me in the ass."

"It's accurate, though! Every rich person that didn't turn into a Stargazer started off with a big advantage. You know, extra food or a bigger bunker. Probably not doin' so well now," Lucy said.

"I lucked out with this place. Was so busy looking in the rearview I didn't even pay attention to what was in front of me. Total accident we ended up here," Henry said.

"Well, why don't you show me to *our* room?" Lucy said, hooking her arm inside Henry's.

He stuttered, skin prickling, "I uh ..."

"Oh, I'm just havin' fun with you. Wanted to see if I still had it, you know? Hey, we had some celebrities come through the hotel and, well, you'd be surprised the heads I could turn with a little sugar in my voice and a loose button."

"Oh yeah?"

"Let's just say wouldn't need more than one degree to get to Kevin Bacon."

Doc took over the kitchen and seemed to become a different person entirely. He hummed but rarely spoke more than a few words, and those always to himself.

"Remarkable!" he said, returning from the cellar with a bottle of wine, furry with dust.

Penny and Michael worked on a puzzle in the living room as Misfit and Gunny, exhausted from their hour-long introduction, napped nose to nose on an overstuffed loveseat. Lucy, who had decided to move in without it having been offered, left to collect her belongings. Henry and Jean resumed their interrupted conversation in the dining room. She lowered her voice to just above a whisper, recounting the moments following their separation.

"I don't think she was there. Now, there's a lot I know, a lot I've been told about what happened to us, to them. But that's a detail I've never nailed down. So, I can just say I hope it's true. If it isn't, then what happened was a mercy and I'm only glad you weren't around to see it."

"Jean, if you're worried about me thinking you're responsible ..." Henry began.

"I know you don't. None of this is our fault. I know that now more than ever. And if that had been Marcus out there you would have done the same."

"I would have."

"But Henry, I gotta tell you. There's a reason I'm excited about us being together again. Yes, I missed havin' someone to talk to. I missed Penny. And I love Michael, Gunny, and the rest."

Jean sat up in her chair. Her head moved in such a natural way, facing him at just the right angle.

"Look, I gotta feed this to you in nibbles, just like I was fed. Too big of a bite might choke you. You know? But I'm excited. I'm excited Henry. I missed you two, and I'm glad we're back together. But it's more than that. Back in the motel I thought at least I'd have someone to bury me when I died. Kinda morbid, but I was in that room by myself for a while. I still had Marcus's blood under my fingernails. I guess I was goin' a little crazy. What I didn't know then, didn't know when I was prowlin' the desert lookin' for you, was the reason for it all. That's too big a bite for now, but there is a reason we're together."

"Dinner in fifteen!" Doc called from the kitchen.

Henry held onto his question as Michael glided through the dining room, unlit cigarette pinched between his teeth and a trail of puzzle pieces clinging to the underside of his forearm.

"You know I trust you, but this kind of talk makes me a little anxious. I feel like you're about to try to sell me a timeshare."

"Ha! *You're* the one with the sweet set-up here. You should be sellin' me. No, no timeshare. No, I didn't join a cult. I truly lost my eyes in the accident. I didn't, like, sacrifice them. I just want you to know, based on what *I* know, we're not passengers. We have a role in what comes next."

Henry licked his lips and swallowed. Jean held up a hand and nodded as if understanding the direction his thoughts were heading.

"Okay, that sounded very cult-like. It's not meant to be. I'm the same old Jean, minus the eyes. Just think back to January. Imagine we were friends then. How crazy would you have thought me tellin' you almost the whole human race would be gone in weeks? That they would destroy almost everything before goin'?"

"I don't think you–"

"Hold on just a sec. Let me get to my point and then you can decide how you wanna finish that sentence."

"Okay."

"Stay with me, okay? Let's work backwards with *ifs*. If Marcus hadn't gone into that store he wouldn't have been killed. I wouldn't have been there when *you* showed up. If we'd gone together, we both would be dead. You might've met me as a body on the floor. If I hadn't killed that man in the grocery store, he might've killed you. There's lots of *ifs*. And it works both ways. If they hadn't become Stargazers. The big *if*, the one that matters to this conversation, is if I hadn't lost my eyes."

Henry scrutinized the lines of her face. There was nothing manic in her smile, and she appeared far more relaxed than he felt.

"If I hadn't lost my eyes I would not have seen. I could not have seen the truth in what I was told."

Michael raced past, a gust of tobacco-scented air following, "Don't finish without me!"

"I won't!" Penny replied.

Henry watched Michael turn the corner into the living room, then turned his attention to Jean. The scar at the end of her stump was crude, an X drawn by a child just learning their letters, somewhere between brown and purple in color. He did not know what was behind her glasses. In the sunlight he caught glimpses, enough to know she was telling the truth about her condition. Not that he questioned it. He had not questioned a thing about her until that moment.

A parade of *ifs* trailed behind him, many from before the word stargazer had a second definition. His fingers danced over the raised flesh beneath his shirt, scars he earned fighting a battle he had not chosen. Jean's smile faltered as she read into Henry's silence.

"I know how-"

"No, Jean," he said, tenting his hand over hers. "I don't understand. Not yet. But I trust you. Just promise me I don't have to go blind too."

She laughed and mimed wiping sweat from her forehead.

"You had me worried! But, no, I'm not making any promises."

———

Penny's head bobbed, half-lidded eyes aimed at the crackling fire. A ring of chocolate encircled her mouth, marshmallow residue like melted cheese connecting her parted lips. Her hands cradled her belly, partly from the discomfort of accommodating so much food. Also, because her sticky fingers were glued to the fabric of her shirt.

It was the biggest meal they'd eaten since the world ended. Doc coaxed complex flavors from dusty jars of preserved vegetables and sauces. He mixed fresh ingredients into the dishes, ground herbs harvested from his own garden. Despite having only a two-burner portable grill to work with, the result was more than impressive, like something off a menu Henry would point at rather than attempt to pronounce. Penny ate without speaking, only pausing to catch her breath between bites. Michael, whose apocalypse diet consisted mostly of food he could chew while still clenching a cigarette, held food in his cheeks when he was too full to swallow it.

Henry, reclined in his chair with his jeans unbuttoned, mentioned all the fixings for s'mores were in the pantry. With much groaning and grimacing, the party migrated outside and got a fire started. Misfit and Gunny slept on the porch, bellies strained from table scraps freely given by all diners.

"I think he's asleep," Henry said, nodding toward Michael.

The cigarette between his index and middle fingers was half ash. Michael's chin rested on his sternum, the visor of his Texas Rangers baseball cap hiding his eyes.

Lucy said, "Reminds me of that scene from The Shining. You know, with the wife when she's talkin' forever and holdin' her cigarette up?"

"That scene was terrifying, Worse than the twins for sure."

"You know, it'd take a lot to scare us now. I mean, after all the shit we've seen. I remember some night shifts at the hotel bein' scared dumb by a flickering light. You know what I used to do? When I was walkin' down a dark hallway I would wink. So, if they, the ghosts or whatever, saw they would know that *I knew* they were there. Like they couldn't get me because I was in on it."

"Sometimes when Marcus was out on a long haul, I'd have full conversations with him out loud like he was in the room with me," Jean said.

"In Afghanistan, I'd have the conversations in my head. Couldn't have people think I was crazy, although I was halfway there," Henry said, his gaze following the smoke to the stars.

He rarely spoke the name aloud, substituting words like *over there*. It had power, that name. *Over there* was a gray place, out of focus as if viewed through a smudged camera lens. Speaking it then, he did not feel the same dread, the same sense that the life he lived in the years since he took off the uniform for the last time were a lie. That he had conjured Penny while dreaming, limbless in a military hospital attached to machines that did his body's work.

"You don't talk about it much, huh?" Lucy said.

Henry shook his head, "Talked about it too much for too long. I just didn't talk about it with the right people, you know? People who didn't have half a dozen other broken men waiting for their turn."

The conversation fizzled, and Henry felt responsible. He stood and adjusted Penny, her dreaming fingers clasping together in a knot on his back.

"I should probably ..."

"Go ahead, Henry. But come back, would you?" Jean said.

He glanced at the house and then at the faces of the strangers around the fire.

"Stay with her as long as you need. I understand your hesitancy. I do. But this has to do with what we were talkin' about before dinner. You trusted me back at the motel. I'm askin' you to trust me tonight."

Henry nodded slowly. He trusted Jean and her judgement of the company she kept. Letting go of Penny, even briefly and at a short distance, was more than a concern for her safety. They were inseparable. Who was he without her? What thoughts might step out from the shadows when not fixated on her safety?

"I'll be back," he said.

"I'm gonna get this one settled," Lucy said, standing and shaking the pins and needles from her legs. "Wake up Michael!"

Henry hoped Penny would wake when he placed her on the bed. If she was awake, he needed to be there. She snored through Henry pulling her shoes and socks off, tucking the sheet around her, wiping the marshmallow residue from her mouth and hands. She smacked her lips as he swept hair from her cheek then rolled on her side showing him her back.

He moved to the window. The glowing embers grew brighter as the breeze picked up. Jean sat with her good had cradling her stump on her lap, head turned away from the dwindling flames. The chairs were empty. Doc retired moments after Lucy escorted Michael to the bedroom he claimed earlier. The vacant chair beside Jean was his. Henry knew he would not be the same person after taking it. While waiting to board the rotator bound for Germany and then Afghanistan, he had a similar thought. It was like a blank page right in the middle of his story, a moment of nothingness before everything came undone.

***

"She asleep?" Jean asked, facing the crunch of his approaching footsteps.

"Didn't wake up even when I tried. Thought I could avoid whatever's about to happen, but Penny had other plans. What about the others?"

Henry took the chair next to Jean, poked the logs in the fire pit sending sparks spiraling skyward.

"Gone to bed. This isn't for them. Doc and Lucy understand as well as I do. Michael understands more than he lets on, I think. This is for you, Henry."

"Has it begun?"

Jean turned away, "Shortly. I'll be honest with you. Your introduction will be different than mine. Mine came on the heels of somethin' I could not explain. There's an element to the crash I left out. Suffice it to say, I woke up knowin' a bit more than you do right now. You mentioned the lights? The ones Penny saw?"

"Yes. I think I'd seen 'em before, off in the distance. Some nights I had trouble sleeping and I'd just stare out the window.

Thought maybe they were flashlights, although that didn't explain the color."

"I saw 'em too. Hopefully won't put an image in your mind, but my place before Doc's was the temporary sort. Meanin' we did our business outside. I can't hold it like I used to, so I became acquainted with the sounds and shapes of the night. Saw the lights way off a couple times. Didn't have a clue what they were. Didn't wanna know to tell the truth."

"And now?"

"Now?"

"What do you think about them?"

Firelight cooled on Jean's face. She removed her sunglasses and squeezed the bridge of her nose. Henry worried she was going to show him what was beneath the strips of white tape sealing her eyes shut.

"Never needed glasses before. Not all the time anyway. These things feel like they weigh ten pounds by the end of the day," she said, smiling. "Back to your question, Henry. Just hang onto it a moment if you don't mind."

Jean placed her good hand atop his, fingers splayed and straining. He understood the gesture to mean she both wanted him to stay but anticipated he would attempt to leave.

He heard it before he saw, a whisper quiet shift of desert soil beneath paws meant for stealth. Henry sat taller in his chair, neck like a periscope. He glanced over his shoulder and saw the darkened window beyond which Penny lay sleeping. He felt exposed and alone despite his company. There were no weapons near, only crumbling logs and a charred stick he'd used to stir them.

"What is ..." Henry trailed off.

It was Gunny, just outside of the fire's light. His eyes glowed, but brighter than they should have, as if the light was generated from within rather than reflected.

"Jean?"

No, not Gunny. It was something else. Her grip on his arm tightened as he angled his body away. The animal trotted into the halo of light, and Henry recognized it at once as a coyote. But there was something uncoordinated in its gait, as if one leg was shorter than the other three. It stuttered with each step.

"What the fu ..." Henry said.

It was not snarling, had not made a sound beyond the muffled crunch of its paws, but its teeth showed, seemingly all of them.

"Its mouth is all, um, wrong."

Jean gripped tighter, her head following the animal's movement around the fire, which revealed more of the devastation to its body. The tail was broken in half, like two bananas left in the bunch. Clots of fur had fallen off its midsection exposing perforated skin, flashes of rib bones. Henry leaned forward and grabbed the stick as the animal stopped.

"What is it doing?" Henry asked, more to himself than Jean.

The coyote sat on its haunches as if waiting for Henry to make the next move.

"Jean, what is this?"

"It's okay. Just watch."

The coyote stood on its hind legs. It stretched its ruined torso, teeth like silver moonlight. The strange, twin lanterns of its eyes scanned the heavens.

"What's it doing?" Henry said as the animal convulsed, shaking loose patches of fur. Its rotted tail severed.

The mouth opened wide enough to swallow an apple whole, then a bowling ball, tendons snapping like overworked leather. A lantern light emerged from the putrefied maw, a miniature, amber sun. The coyote crumpled, a corpse once again.

A man stepped out from the shadows, two hands held up as if he meant to grasp the suspended orb.

"This animal is not alive. And this," the man said, hands framing the light. "This yearns to be something it cannot. It must not."

Henry was halfway to standing, held in place by Jean. "Who are you?"

Instead of answering, the man twirled his hands as if spinning cotton candy between them. He clasped them together, paused, then ripped them apart. The amber light split in two and followed the paths the man indicated as if strapped to rockets, diminishing to nothing in an instant.

"I am Ted. I have many names, and we have much time before us to speak them all. I am a friend of Jean if that helps soothe your mind."

Henry returned to his seat but did not release his grip on the stick.

"I don't understand."

The man smiled. "Jean speaks those words so often I forget their meaning."

He strolled around the fire pit and extended a hand. Only then did Jean release her hold. Ted's hand was as hard as granite, and Henry had to grit his teeth to keep from seething.

"Jean requested I not speak anything that would confuse you. I will try not to. I am happy to meet you, Henry, father of Nickel. It is not the first time we have met, just the first time you are aware of it."

Apocalypse Radio

It's Maurice again. I have not heard from CK. We are still within the window of time he hoped to return from his expedition to the monument, though at the upper limit of it. I hope the delay has a more benign explanation than my prejudiced inklings. I had not planned to broadcast over what I consider to be *his* airwaves. For our differences, which are few, he has done more to unite the fragmented populace than any I know of.

The airwaves are busy now. Maybe I'll carve out my own niche, create a little space for myself. Maybe I'll name it something more hopeful. Balance, you know?

But not until I hear from CK, or enough time has passed I know that is no longer a possibility.

A bit of news to share and on what might be my last gig hosting Apocalypse Radio. I hope it is. I hope the next time you tune in it is CK's voice, not mine.

West Coast Annie, as she calls herself, made it to Nevada. She's determined to break into Area 51, though she's having trouble finding it. Can you imagine what it was like there when the excrement hit the fan? All these folks with Top Secret clearances walking through layers of security to stand outside and gaze at the stars? Probably thought it was an attack of some sort, until there was no one left to think it. West Coast Annie says she found ruins, evidence of humanity in the vicinity. She thinks the entrance might be beneath the rubble, which is too heavy for her to move.

If you're in the area and have access to a crane ...

A Japanese fishing boat washed up on a beach in Oregon. What *was* Oregon, anyway. I guess I can stop making that observation. We all know what used to be. There was no crew. Jake, who has no nickname, is requesting assistance from anyone who can read Japanese, as he found a journal sealed in a plastic bag in the captain's quarters. He does not believe the boat was abandoned by Stargazers. He thinks they were refugees attempting to cross the ocean, to see if things were different here. Perhaps anticipating the language barrier, the final few pages of the journal were drawings. Crude but understandable. If you're in the area or passing through and know the language, well, be sure to let us know what it says.

(sighs)

These, uh, updates, these stories stand on their own legs. They are interesting and worthy of your attention. I know it's tough out there. For some of you, depending on your circumstances, this may be your last exposure to this broadcast. I hope it gives you comfort to know we will go on.

These stories are also a Trojan horse, of sorts. I have another update, another story to share. For those who would prefer a sense of nostalgia, of the fantastic, you can power down now. My story is of the fantastic, but not in a Frodo and Sam on an adventure way. It was an adventure that came to me. Was I the intended audience? And through me to you? I do not know. Feels like just ... one of those things.

I live in what passed for nature in another life. Mostly evergreen trees, pretty to look at, but no real character. A forest neutered of its threats; its teeth filed to blunt edges. The wildlife, save for a wayward apex predator, is inconsequential. Deer and rodents fulfilling their downscaled role in the circle of life. It's what we have allowed to live, a zoo with less obvious borders.

(sighs)

Feels like I have a vendetta against the forest, doesn't it? I assure you I do not. I have loved living in this little abode for a decade or more. I suppose old grievances are surfacing, that part of me that longed to have an adventure, to trick a troll into turning to stone and mingle with elves. Maybe that is still to come. It's an awfully big world out there, now.

In my hidden corner of the forest there are the expected fauna. Deer, as I mentioned. Raccoons and coyotes. I do not know the names of the birds but consider myself lucky to have seen an owl. More common than fleas, though, are squirrels. So many goddamn squirrels I'm convinced my mind doesn't even register them anymore. There could be one in the room with me right now, and I would never know.

I jest. I do not dislike them. They're just sort of unremarkable. Tell the next person you meet you saw a squirrel and see what reaction you don't get. Having said that, I am familiar with the squirrels around my house. I've had a lot of time to stare out the window since, oh, about the first week of February. Saw Martha staring at the stars through this very window in front of me.

But we don't have to get into that.

Martha had a different opinion about the squirrels. Maybe it was a redirected maternal instinct. Maybe she was a squirrel in another life.

She fed the squirrels. Not Disney-style out of her hand. She filled a small bowl with nuts and slices of vegetables she did not foresee surviving to make our dinner table and placed it in view of the breakfast nook where she took her coffee.

Martha is no longer here, though it feels like she is some days. I haven't touched her clothes, except to smell them. Each time, there's a little less of her in the fabric. Her nightstand is just as she left it, reading glasses parked next to her favorite Robert McCammon book. The spine's so broken you can't read the title. I'll never get over losing her, but you do move on in your own way and in your own time.

Part of my healing process has been, you guessed it, goddamn squirrels. Next to the McCammon book was the bowl of nuts ready for a morning that never came. I'll have to correct myself here. Her nightstand is untouched save for the removal of the bowl. I have taken the mantle of Feeder of Squirrels. I am not fascinated by them as she was, but it is fun to watch them pack their cheeks.

I named one "Mama" for reasons that should be obvious. I was happy to see her. Figured it took one thing off her plate not to have to worry about food. She's easy to spot, even when her belly returned to its normal size. There's a little triangular chip out of her left ear. Line up one million squirrels and I could pick her out every time. Mama comes almost every morning. The mornings I don't see her I will leave extra nuts outside in the afternoon.

Going to have to take a side road for a moment, then we'll come back to Mama. We've talked about the lights. I wager talking about them has done little to strengthen our understanding, but at least we know the phenomenon is not conjured. I wondered that myself the first time I saw them. We know what they can do and suspect what they are aiming to do. They can reanimate dead animals, restore temporary vigor to parched muscles. That is not the final goal, to become a corpse. The lights follow the living. For lack of a better explanation, they want to get inside.

We think. No one knows. None have succeeded to my knowledge.

For all the squirrels I do not see, for all I have forgotten, I see Mama. I look for her every day. As I said, I know her by her shadow alone.

This was a few days ago. It's taken me that long to gather my thoughts. Mama ate well that morning. I recall her standing like a prairie dog, cheeks stretched to their limits. It felt like she saw me through the glass. I started thinking about Martha, wondering if it was a sign. When I came to, Mama was gone. It was a good thing. A sad and happy thing.

Later that day, just before true dark, I saw fireflies on the porch, hovering over the approximate area of the nut bowl. I realized I forgot to retrieve it, and so I walked to the back door to do so.

Just enough light. There was *just* enough for me to see the outline of her form, the silhouette of her ear with the triangular cutout. I saw this. I saw *her*. I knew it was Mama. But there were lights in her eyes. Some color between amber and brown.

I saw a raven with eyes like that, one wing missing, hobbling on matchstick legs. That is in harmony with what we know about these lights, with what has been shared over these airwaves. But Mama was alive just hours before. My days tend to bleed together, but I did not confuse that morning with another. She filled her cheeks and I thought of Martha.

Is the suggestion obvious? Mama either met an untimely demise within hours of our parting, or she didn't. Her death would have been subtle, an attack vigorous enough to kill her but not so brutal as to make the devastation obvious. Because she was whole, friends. She appeared to be alive, to have never died. And if that's true ... well I haven't quite wrapped my mind around the implications.

In failing, they learn. They try again. Perhaps they succeed with a rodent, a mouse or squirrel like Mama. What comes next?

(sighs)

I stopped putting nuts out. I haven't seen Mama, and I hope not to. Something new to fear, friends. Now and forever. Always something new to fear.

Chapter Ten

I Will Answer What I Can

October

"How far is it again?" Henry asked.

He leaned against a porch pillar, steam leaking from his nostrils. Curtains of mist hid the alpine desert vista. He searched his memory for an obscure adage about beginning a journey in the fog. Surely sailors advised against it. Though it would be tenuous, he needed something, something with teeth, something to delay the inevitable another day.

"I do not understand your measurements. If we are not interrupted, we should arrive in five days," Ted replied.

Henry nodded and slowly pivoted. He found it difficult to dispute Ted directly and relied on Jean for that purpose.

"I can feel you lookin' at me. You know it's gotta happen. Penny will be fine. Doc is here'n Lucy's a better shot than you," she said.

He was nervous about leaving Penny, was more inclined to bring her along. Ted dismissed the notion with a flick of his wrist, as if sending an overdone steak back to the kitchen.

"This is for your wisdom, not hers. She has her own lessons. Your paths are like a braid, but they will not end in the same place," Ted told him.

The journey was the final "chunk" of the puzzle, according to Ted. A not small part of Henry did not want to understand more than he did, to have the foundations of his worldview further eroded. There might not be much left to stand on, he feared, and that was a thin place to begin with.

"It's just ..." Henry began, his hands like a hamster's wheel. "It's just this has all been building toward something. It feels like it."

"And?" Jean said.

"And it wasn't easy to make it this far," Henry said, then ran his fingers through his hair. "So, what comes next must be terrifying."

For a moment no one spoke. There were sounds from inside. Doc preparing breakfast and Penny attempting to train Misfit to sit for a morsel of egg.

Jean nodded. "It's true. It was terrifying for me so many times back in the RV. The lights in the desert, the headlights too. I fell asleep every night thinkin' it was for the last time. That someone would find us. And the worst thought was havin' to see Michael taken out before me. And anyway, you won't get pity from me 'cause you've still got your eyes."

"You can't keep using that. I didn't attack you. Something else did."

"Grow me some new ones and I'll stop."

Henry pressed a fist to his lips, attempting to stifle laughter.

"What about you?" he said, turning his attention to Michael. For the moment, Michael was preoccupied with his pipe, the lighter's flame seemingly repelled by the tobacco in the bowl. Cigarette supplies had begun to dwindle. There was enough for the near future, but not for forever. Doc suggested pipes after one thousand previous suggestions to quit smoking altogether were rebuffed.

Michael abandoned his efforts, plucking the pipe from his teeth long enough to say, "Me? I'm the muscle!"

Henry coughed as if someone had gut punched him, unable to subdue the laughter, which passed to Jean while Ted gazed into the mist as if he was seeing through it. Several aftershocks followed the initial eruption, the laughter's strength fading each time like thunder from a departing storm. Henry leaned against the pillar and gripped the seizing muscles below his ribs.

"Oh," Jean said, dabbing her cheeks. "I didn't know I could still cry. Thank you, Michael."

"He just gets to hang and smoke, and I have to walk two-hundred miles with a god?" Henry said.

"Oh no. Michael has his own trainin' to do," Jean replied. "You can't see it, but I'm winkin' under my eye patch."

Michael reclined in his chair and smiled as a smoke ring dissipated before him.

"Are you prepared?" Ted asked.

Henry shook his head, "It'd be a lie to say yes. Out of curiosity, though, what happens if I say no?"

Ted showed the palm of one hand, then shrugged almost imperceptibly, "Then I would wait."

Henry sighed, "I guess I should say my goodbyes, then. You gonna put on a shirt?"

Ted frowned, "I am wearing pants. Is that not enough?"

"You know, it's really tough to pick a fight with you."

"Jean tells me the same."

Penny hugged her father from the side, one eye on the egg quivering on the tines of her fork. Misfit swept her tail beneath it, the fur of her face speckled yellow.

"Listen to Jean, okay?"

"Okay, Dad."

Over the past few months, Penny began to drop the *-dy* off the word *Daddy*. Unprompted to his knowledge, a subtle change that felt like someone had taken a potato peeler to his heart.

"And Doc and Lucy."

"Okay," she said, pulling away.

"Love you. I'll be back before you know it."

Penny kneeled on the floor, fork above her head and the other hand patting the floor. Henry mussed her hair, hiked his backpack higher on his shoulders, and exited the house. Ted, who wore no backpack, clapped Henry on the back.

"Look! The sun has joined us."

"Great."

They descended the porch steps together, Henry casting backward glances as he walked. He expected to see Penny's face in the window, but she was trapped in her fixation. Her passions burned bright but beyond the present preoccupation there was another burning brighter. Jean said she was like a butterfly in a field of wildflowers, and the most enticing petals were always just ahead.

"Do not worry for them. They are protected. Vida is watching them."

"I didn't see her."

"And neither would any jester wishing to harm Nickel!"

"Penny."

"Your names are difficult to know."

Ted stopped at the soft summit of a hill offering a panoramic view interrupted by steppes to the northeast and mountains to the west. As the mist retreated, it left behind silver teardrops on the foliage, leaves a shade between green and gray. Gunny sampled them and moved on, trotting down the hill as if he knew their destination.

"Why is that? You've filled my ears to overflowing, but I don't think you ever explained it."

Ted made a grand, sweeping gesture with his hand.

"Are there supposed to be words to go along with that?" Henry asked.

"A long while ago, there were people here. They did not stay many days because there was not much water. A long while before that there was more water, and there were more people. A long while before that I was in a different place with different people, another place before that, another before that. Back and back. I can see their faces. Some smiling. Some in fear. Some with war paint showing teeth. Some gray with ash."

Ted nodded and began walking.

Henry remained a moment longer.

"Wait. That's the end? You forgot the, uh, ending," Henry said.

He jogged to catch up as Gunny galloped into the distance, tail on high alert.

"There are too many names. Your white dog?" Ted said, pointing. "I have met thousands of white dogs. Gray dogs. Black dogs. Many brown. Thousands of names. Hundreds of languages. Languages that shifted over time. Some names were so large you could not speak them in one breath. I have concluded learning names."

The crunch of desert soil beneath their shoes filled the gap in conversation. Henry glanced over his shoulder but the recently conquered hill blocked his view of the earthen features surrounding the house. Penny was there. She was safe. The path ahead was a mystery.

"What about Jean? You know her name."

Ted stopped, rocks skidding underfoot.

"That is different."

"How?"

"It is easy because she is always wearing jeans."

"We have said many words together, but there are many more you have not spoken. You have questions. I will answer what I can."

Following their nocturnal introduction, Ted redirected focus from Jean to Henry. Jean was grateful for the mental respite, said she could finally *think my own damn thoughts again*. Together, occasionally accompanied by one or both dogs, Ted and Henry walked around the property and spoke of the end of the world.

"So, it wasn't aliens?" Henry told Jean after the first session. "Well, not in the way we thought, huh?"

"What do you mean?"

"Oh, you haven't made it that far yet."

The conversations were mostly one-sided, save for Henry's frequent requests for Ted to repeat himself. It was a combination of Ted's strange language habits and the information he attempted to convey. Over the days and weeks, Henry thought of hundreds of questions. So many he had little room in his mind for other thoughts. But none surfaced at Ted's invitation. Not satisfied with his explanation of memorizing names, the pair pursued the topic until Ted began to sing songs in other languages leaving no space for debate.

Part of Henry's consternation was in not grasping the limits of Ted's knowledge. He understood Ted and his ilk were once gods. They were now something different. He also understood they had been present on Earth for a long time, though Ted quickly grew frustrated when Henry attached numbers to concepts of *time*.

"You start counting your years at *one* like there were not thousands of years of history before it," Ted said.

"Whoa whoa. *I* didn't. They were almost up to two thousand by the time I was born."

Ted narrowed his gaze. He brushed a thin curtain of silver hair from his face, nostrils flaring.

"You did not, but your fathers did. I can smell them. I can smell them in your blood."

Henry smiled, his empty belly announcing itself.

"Ted, that's the strangest thing anyone has ever told me. Considering what we've talked about in the past couple of months, that's sayin' something."

Ted shrugged, turned to the east and began singing. The hills diminished in height. Occasionally, Ted would stop singing to share a story, pointing at an unremarkable patch of earth that once hosted a battle between a brown bear and a saber-toothed tiger. The conflict ended in a draw, but the cat's injury impeded its ability to hunt, and it died weeks later. The bear, Ted said, lived a long life for a bear, siring many cubs.

"His blood is gone, now. There are no brown bears here."

"Will there be?"

Ted nodded, "Probably. They will fill the spaces you leave behind."

The sun was well behind them then, the sky just beginning to darken to the east. Between Henry and the horizon, at a distance of maybe a mile, there was a single white mote upon the brown of the earth. Gunny charged into the desert as if he might wake tomorrow to find himself in his post card-sized backyard, the previous seven months just a strange dream. His enthusiasm for exploration, for chasing the fading aroma of cattle dogs dead or displaced, was sturdier than the legs that carried him. His tail flicked as if shooing flies, but he would travel no further unless carried.

"Looks like a good place to stop," Henry said, pointing ahead. "You gonna eat?"

"Maybe. And, yes, it is a good place. It is hours until sleep, and you have not offered a question worth answering."

"Not easy to do with your singin' taking up all the air."

"You could request me to stop."

"Would you?"

"Some songs must be finished. Others can be interrupted."

"How do I know the difference?"

"Simply ask. If I do not stop singing, you have your answer."

"I'm ready for bed," Michael said, stretching and yawning to emphasize the point.

"That's where you're goin' next. Just be patient," Jean said.

"For what?"

"Well, if I tell you this whole thing's a waste, now, isn't it?"

"I'm shruggin'," Michael said.

"I can hear it."

Had Henry emerged from the darkness then, he could have credibly accused the pair of not having moved the entire day. Michael sat in the same chair holding the same disappointing pipe. Jean sat beside him, unchanged except for smiles of increasing frequency and a haze of wine burps around her. Michael's "training" would not have been obvious as such to an outside observer. It looked more like a conversation.

"There's mosquitoes," Michael complained.

"I heard pipe smoke keeps 'em away."

For the next ten minutes, Michael turned his attention to the pipe, the contents of the bowl and flame of the lighter repelling each other. Jean sank deeper into her chair, wine bottle secure between her legs. The god protecting them, called Vida, was not engaging like Ted. In fact, she did not speak at all.

"She communicates through dance," Doc had said. "Though I can't say I understand it as yet."

"Well, that's just perfect for a blind woman. Maybe I can feel the wind of her skirt flarin' and translate for you," Jean replied.

She was not so helpless. In fact, she *saw* Vida more clearly than any of the gods, including Ted.

Jean pointed. "Over there. What do you see?"

Michael squinted and held a hand over his eyes as if he was gazing at the sun.

"Uh, nothin' I think. There somethin' out there I'm s'posed to see?"

"You sure you don't see anything?"

Michael sighed for effect and grunted as he pushed himself out of the chair. He stood at the edge of the porch and leaned his weight against a square column. He folded his arms, face pinched and eyes searching.

"There's just some lightning bugs out there."

"Lightning bugs?"

"Yeah, a few of 'em."

"What color are they?"

Another pause. Michael's instinct was to say *yellow*, as that was the typical color when the insect flashed.

"Kinda orange? Brown maybe?"

Jean smirked. "You ever see a brown lightning bug?"

Michael shook his head, "I'm shakin' my head."

"I can hear it. Okay, how 'bout this one. You know that strange lady that doesn't speak? The one who's supposed to be watchin' over us while Ted's away?"

"Vida?"

"Where do you think she is right now? And, before you say I don't know, just think about it."

He stared for a while, unsure where he should be looking.

"Can I have a cigarette?"

"After."

Michael jogged down the steps and stood on the front lawn. The stubbled earth poked through his moccasins, but the lure of a cigarette clouded the faint pain signal. He had only seen her a couple times in the daylight, off in the distance sitting on a boulder. So much of what he used to know about the world had come undone that year the addition of a mute, dancing god almost went unnoticed. He faced the house, the windows dark save for a pale glow from Lucy's room. She stayed up listening to the radio most nights. It wasn't music, though. Sounded like people talking.

Penny was asleep and Misfit was probably curled up beside her with egg in her fur. Doc was also an *early to bed* sort. Michael thought this was so he could wake up before everyone else in the house and make fun of them for being *lazy*. His room did not face the front yard, but Michael knew he was asleep. Did Vida ever go inside? He didn't recall seeing her there, but his concentration had mostly been directed at his pipe bowl recently.

He turned with the same sharpness as if someone had whispered his name.

"This is gonna sound silly but try to not see her with your eyes."

Very little sounded silly to Michael, but he didn't hear Jean's advice. He rubbed his forearms, fingers of cool air like silk tickling his skin. He crunched over the grass that never turned green no matter how much attention Doc gave it.

"Over there?" he said, pointing.

Jean could not see where Michael indicated, but that didn't matter.

"Can you see her?"

"Um ..."

"If you had to call it by a color, what would you say?"

It was too dark to be certain, even with the house to orient him, but Michael thought she was on the little hill with the bench and memorial stones. He went there to talk to his mom. It felt weird the first few times, but then it became part of his every day, like picking up Gunny's poop.

"Purple."

Jean smiled and downed the wine.

"That's good, Michael. Trainin's done for today."

The world had never felt so big, its borders limitless. In his life before, before the world ended and before *penny* meant something other than a coin he would not take the time to pluck off a sidewalk, he felt something close. A thousand mountains he could not name if granted an eternity to do so, their white peaks like the froth of frozen waves. During quiet moments, Henry thought of walking away, of unburdening himself of his equipment and the obligations that accompanied it. Walk away and keep walking until his will left him. He would never be found. He would become earth again, a temporary barnacle on an anonymous mountain broken down into primordial el-ements by sun and snow.

"You have not asked the necessary questions," Ted said.

Henry shook his head and glanced over the flames. For a moment, the chill in the air felt like a mountain breeze.

"You aren't exactly helpful, you know? Half the questions I do ask you say it's not time for."

Ted held up a hand, "I will tell you the answer, and then I will tell you the question you should have asked."

Henry almost replied with sarcasm but stopped himself.

"Go for it."

Ted's Story, Part One

You see the stars above you in all directions. Those you can see are but a small fragment of your Milky Path, which is just one of many Milky Paths. There are more Milky Paths than there are stars in your Milky Path. This is what steals your eye. As a tree will steal your eye if there are no others around. A cloud will steal your eye if it is alone in the sky.

There are universes hidden within universes. The Great Un-seen, some name it. Between us and the moon, the sun, the planets there is nothing. That is what you see. Nothing. Between your sun and the stars, between the Milky Path and other Milky Paths, there is nothing.

This is a lie. There is nothing between you and me, no tethers, yet we are connected. There is nothing between you and … Penny, yet you are connected. A grain of sand in the desert is not connected to you. Or is it? It touches the air that touches your face. If it is hidden below, it touches a grain of sand above, which touches another, which touches another, and on and on. The same is truthful for the Universe.

Dream of a spiderweb trapped between two flowers. Can you see it? When a fly touches the web, the spider knows at once. It vibrates. It causes ripples like a pebble thrown into a pond. Now dream of not one spiderweb but many, and in all directions. The silk goes to forever. If a fly touches the web the spider knows, no matter how far away it is. Distance is a lie.

Henry: Who are the spiders?

It is too early to name them "who." Some may be who. Others are what.

Henry: What?

Your language is troublesome. I know other languages not so troublesome, but you do not know those words.

In the Universe there are living things, dead things, and things that have never lived. If life is the shore, then dead things are the waves that can touch it for a time, but the ocean will never let them stay. They must always return. Life is the fly in the spiderweb. Life is the pebble in the pond. But not any fly and not any pebble. It must be …

Henry: Special?

I do not like that word but cannot think of one better.

The Great Unseen is not one place but many places and many possibilities. Dream of a ladder. You are on what some name the third step.

Henry: Me, specifically?

Your kind. Most of the flies are below you. You cannot even see them now, and not many spiders are interested. The third step is ... important. It is a boulder in the pond. Do you understand?

Henry: No.

I do not like your measurements of time, but we can say it was a long time ago that your kind reached the third step. A long time as you understand time. This was a boulder in the pond. This sent the silk to trembling.

That is when we came. Not right away, but not long after. To remember. To watch. Could your kind reach the fourth step? It was not our aim to interfere, but we fell in love. Not as a man and woman love, more like a parent and child. You were not our children, but we felt ...

Henry: Obligated?

I do not know what that word means. It is like with Jean and white dog. Jean was not white dog's master, but she could not let him wander once she found him. Yes, he might have triumphed. He might have become the king of dogs. He might have died alone and hungry.

Henry: Obligated is the right word. So, *you* were the spiders?

We were the who spiders, not the what. Other who spiders came and left. They did not fall in love. The who spiders had names before we came here. The what spiders did not. Do you understand?

Henry: The what spiders have never been alive?

Yes! But they are also not dead. Dream of the ocean again. The waves touch the shore, but they always return to the ocean. The what spiders do not come from the ocean. There is nothing pulling them back. They can walk along the shore, but the shore does not notice them ... in the beginning.

In the beginning the shore does not notice. But after a time, a long time as you understand time, there is an effect. Those spiders have never had a name, have never lived, and it is the only thing they desire. They do not know it as you and I know things, but this desire is as real as the blood in your tubes. They are shadows hoping to become what blocks the light.

The spiders, those with names and without, came from all over. Your kind climbed a step. The vibrations echoed throughout the Universe. There was light in your hearts. After the third step the others are possible.

We did not regard them. We were in love, remember? Even a god can be blind to threats when he is in love. And we did not name them as threats. They were nothing. Unliving. Unnamed. Insignificant, like so much of the Universe. What danger is a shadow, even an infinite number of them?

A long time passed. Time as you understand it.

Before we realized it was happening, the shadows found a way in.

Henry nodded and glanced up from the flames. Ted stood, hands on his hips and eyes scanning the horizon to the north. Silver braids as thick as mooring rope hung to his ribs. He began to sing.

"Wait!" Henry said, standing so fast he sent Gunny barking at the darkness beyond the fire. "What happened next?"

Ted continued singing.

"Ted. Ted you can't do that. I feel like I'm gonna throw up. What happened next?"

Ted sang louder.

"Ted! You said you would tell me the question I should have asked. Can you at least do that?"

Ted sang a final note, held Henry's gaze, then turned his attention back to the horizon.

"You simply should have asked me what question you should be asking. We will speak more tomorrow. Find sleep if you can. Your feet are as soft as cow udders and we have many steps before us."

Chapter Eleven

This is What Matters

Jean tapped her hiking stick. The sound reminded her of one of those drums you play with your fingers.

"Is this the eatin' kind or the carvin' kind?" she said.

With a grunt of effort, Doc snapped the vine with his shears. He leaned his weight against the top of his thigh, sweat pitter-pattering over the bright orange skin.

"Oh, we can do both I suppose. Carved pumpkins won't keep long in this weather, but Penny'll get a kick out of it," he said, then glanced at Lucy. "You gonna do something besides stand there and look pretty?"

"You're a bigger flirt than the geezers at the VFW. I volunteered there for the ego boost. And, no, I'm not doing anything besides standing here 'cause that's what you asked me to do. Hold the wheelbarrow so it don't tip over."

Doc shook his head and waddled to the next gourd.

"How's Michael's trainin' comin' along?" Lucy said.

"Oh, good enough. If I got cigarettes for bait that is."

Lucy pushed the wheelbarrow half a foot then dabbed her brow.

"Still don't understand what y'all are doin'. I don't think he knows either, tell the truth."

Jean inhaled the desert air. There were a thousand little details she would not have noticed before, how the humidity sat in her lungs, more of it in recent days, the slightly bitter scent of the severed pumpkin vine. She smelled Doc's sweat and Lucy's sunscreen above everything else. The odor of burned tobacco was inescapable. It followed Michael everywhere, and for most of the day he was within arm's reach of Jean. She didn't smell it then, just its memory, as that morning Michael became aware of his own funk and decided to take a bath.

"There's different levels of knowin'. Some might be to pass a test, others to wake somethin' up inside. Guess that's what we're workin' on."

Lucy abandoned the wheelbarrow, which was in no danger of tipping over. She stood next to Jean and gave her elbow a little pinch.

"You ever think about airing your eyes out? With my cancer scare I had to keep patches over my skin here and there, where they cut, you know. There wasn't a better feelin' in the world than when I took 'em off the first time."

Jean reflexively touched her sunglasses.

"They do get sweaty. You don't think–."

Lucy interrupted, "With all we seen since January? I mean, wasn't as many people here as the city, but it was enough. That first day had three guests walk off the roof. It's not a far enough drop to kill 'em outright. That's how I was introduced to this whole thing. Found a fella in the stairwell, legs like spaghetti ... with sauce, tryin' to pull himself up to fall off again."

Jean nodded and removed her sunglasses. She turned her head away at the same time.

"Yeah, I know. It's just a bit personal. Michael and Penny knew me before, though they've known me this way a lot longer. Just didn't want to spook 'em."

Lucy hugged her from the side and planted a little peck on her cheek.

"It's kinda funny. We still call 'em eyes even though you ain't got no eyes."

"Hilarious," Jean said, smiling.

Lucy returned to the wheelbarrow as Doc loaded the next pumpkin. Jean pivoted, showing them her back. Doc had seen, of course, but even that had been months ago. The glass had not worked itself out of the eye tissue as Doc had hoped, and he did not have the tools to perform an operation even if he had the skill for it. He worried about infection, about the glass migrating and causing more damage. It was Ted who took her eyes.

"I will not repair them. That path ends in failure. But I can take them away from you," Ted had told her.

"Why failure?"

"There are thousands of paths before you, more than thousands but now is not the time for that. From where you stand they are bunched together, not like a bundle of reeds but like the trunk of an oak. Far ahead of you, in time, the edges blur, paths moving a little from the others. Far far ahead of you, in time, the branches form. Most still going up but some bending east and west."

"Is that the whole answer?"

"The paths where I have repaired your vision end at the same place. Every one."

"Not a good place?"

"Not a good place."

Jean peeled the tape. Not all the way, just one corner. She slipped a finger beneath the pad and lifted it. The breeze was so light it hardly made her hair quiver, but it felt as cool as melting ice on her skin. She repeated the exercise with her other eye as Doc and Lucy bantered behind her. It was not vanity that led her to secure the tape again. That was so far in her rearview mirror she couldn't see it even with perfect vision.

She sensed the paths before her, not as an oak but a shimmering road, an oil-slick rainbow brilliance. Along some paths, she discarded the tape and the pads hiding the hollows of her eyes. They twisted and gnarled away from her, ending prematurely.

The tape and pads were not for her. They were for someone or something *far ahead* of her. Someone or something who would interpret them as weakness.

"What do you think they're doin'?" Lucy said.

Jean put a hand to her chest.

"Jesus, woman, you can move like a mouse when you want to!"

Lucy whispered, "If I sneak away real quiet, Doc don't notice. He forgets I'm around and does the work himself."

Jean shook her head, "I think he'd do it if you just asked him nice."

"Mmhhmm. So, what do you think Penny and, uh, the other one are doin'? Kinda looks like they're dancin' together."

Jean smoothed the tape to her cheeks put her sunglasses back on. She watched them for a while, seeing them in a way only a god would understand. Maybe Michael in time. She smiled, recognizing the interaction between Penny and Vida as a thin, glittering band of her own path. Doc was there, too, adding his own luminescence.

For a time.

For a time, they all were.

But only for a time.

"I think that's exactly what they're doin'."

The landscape shifted from alpine desert to a world in transition. It seemed to be a convergence of multiple environments, none executed successfully. The grass grew in tufts, like a scalp shaved in darkness. The hearty mesquite, roots sipping from a water table far beneath the surface, looked like an eruption of snakes frozen in time. The evergreens were left behind with the change in elevation, the steppes stuttering to blunted hills. It was stark but not in a way that inspired romantic thoughts of loss or new beginnings. No, this land with its paint-flaked oil derricks and nervous cattle who had forgotten the scent of man, stirred old memories of isolation and mania. Henry felt so disconnected from reality *over there*, boredom and confusion always bookended by chaos, he began to wonder if it was real. Did he really exist? Is this really where his decisions had taken him?

How could he ever go home?

The desolation around him felt the same. Was Penny real? Was his silent, shirtless companion truly a dethroned god, or was Henry only then privy to a flash of sanity, one last, desperate kick to the surface?

Gunny trotted beside. There was nothing of interest ahead, apparently, no threats to confront. His tail was no longer alert but bobbing as he sniffed at bushes without pausing to mark them. Ted still sang, but mostly to himself. He shared few stories. There were no memorable battles along the path they walked, just an odd recollection about a jaguar that adopted an orphaned fawn. After relaying the tale, Ted recalled it was a story the tribes used to tell and might not have been based in fact. He stopped sharing stories. He did demolish every fence he encountered, however.

"This is a cruel invention," he had said. Henry did not question it, feeling as though he understood his meaning.

Henry checked his watch, anticipating it was at least early in the afternoon. He was both surprised and disappointed to discover it was only mid-morning. Although he felt the miles behind him in the soles of his feet and ache in his calves, he was also certain there were fewer than he might guess based on those inputs.

"You told me walking was part of it, part of what I needed to learn. I don't feel like I'm learning much but my feet feel like shit. My skin feels like sandpaper. And all of me stinks."

Ted tapped his chin, "How do your feet feel like shit? Have you walked through it? It is quite easy to avoid."

"No. I mean they hurt. It's a … never mind. Should I just ask you what questions I should ask you?"

"Not today. Today we simply walk. There will be questions when we get to where we are going."

"Which is?"

Ted pointed, one eye squinting, "Over there. If we are not interrupted, we should be there before the sun sets."

Their path brought them to a farmhouse showing the effects of nine months without maintenance. The weeds were overgrown, but the yard was a brown wasteland otherwise. There was not enough rainfall to support non-native grass accustomed to the fleeting, uncharitable clouds. An oak tree with a tire swing was close to giving up the ghost, the leaves gray as moth wings and missing from half its branches. The 1980s Ford pickup in the gravel driveway leaned toward a flat tire. Its windows were fuzzy with dust and pollen. Beer cans bleached white by the sun pooled in the tilted bed.

A voyeuristic part of Henry wished to nudge the front door and explore. If not for Penny, he might never have left San Antonio and its tightly packed suburbs. So many homes and stories. He was on the periphery of middle age, though incorporating recent history into the equation would likely complicate the accepted calculus.

It seemed impossible. Middle-aged. He could not help but believe he'd *done it wrong*, somehow, that he'd bluffed his way through adulthood. Seeing how other adults kept their homes was like pulling back the curtain. Did other adults store their liquor on a shelf out in the open, or was that something he should hide?

Their legs dangled off the porch. The wicker chairs appeared to struggle with the dusty pillows they supported and there were no other options for sitting. Gunny inspected the front yard for a few minutes, sampling the air around a plastic slide and toddler-sized picnic table. He blessed them with a trickle then stretched out in the shade of the house, falling asleep within moments.

"So, were you always here? On our side of the world, I mean. Did you move around?" Henry took a bite of a peanut butter and blackberry preserves sandwich. Lucy insisted on packing his food but did not solicit his opinion on what to include. Doc's baking prowess could not match his skill as a cook. The bread crust was as tough as jerky, and Henry's jaw throbbed after a few bites.

"I have been here for a long time. Not in the same place. I was in the jungle for a long time."

"Other tribes?"

Ted began to braid his hair. "Sometimes. Sometimes I simply wandered."

"What about the others?"

"Ina was in what you would call the middle of the east. It was true desert, there, unlike ..." Ted said, then gestured to the land before them. "And she wandered, like me. We all did. She has different names by different people. Some knew her as a god. Others as a magic person."

"A shaman?"

Ted showed his palms, "That is a good enough word. Nadine wandered then came here later like me. Same for her. Different names to different people. She was known as the bringer of seasons. It is a good thing to be known for until one season does not end or another starts too soon. When this happens, the tributes become curses. We do not need your love, but it is different to be hated. Then you move on, become something else. Vida was above Ina, where it is cold.

"Mankind began to change, began to gather around fewer ideas, many of their own creation. For most of your time you were troubled with surviving. When that was not so important you were troubled with power. We were not the gods you needed and so we moved on, became something else."

Henry swished a mouthful of water and wiped his lips.

"What are you now?"

Ted's fingers froze. He tilted his head and pointed his nose at the sky. Henry assumed he was about to be treated to another song.

"We are no longer true desert. We are," Ted said, then gestured before him again. "In between. That is a bigger part to the story. It is the last chapter for what has been written."

"You're not gods?"

Ted shook his head, fingers back at work, "That was your word, not ours. Remember, a ladder can work in both directions."

———

They walked and talked, not about important things. Ted was happy to share memories of his time as a god and Henry's curiosity was ravenous. The miles passed quickly, Henry no longer checking his watch in two-minute intervals. Ted was a living encyclopedia who sometimes sang in dead languages. It was obvious time had not softened his affection for the people he left behind. He smiled when he spoke of them, so wide his eyes were mere slits.

There was something else, hidden within the tales of love and war, of upheaval and peace. A thread of longing, of wistfulness and regret.

"We are almost there," Ted said, coming to a stop. He gestured vaguely to a hill in the distance, dark beneath the waning light of the sun.

Before Henry could again question where *there* was, Ted spoke, "I can see them in you. Your grandfathers, back and back, a long time ago as you understand time. The tribes fell apart, mixed with the conquerors, often not their decision. And so there is some of that in you as well. It is no accident you are standing here. It is no accident Nickel is who she is. It is in her as well."

"What is in her?"

"That," Ted said, then squeezed Henry's shoulder and ushered him forward. "That is the final question. Let us walk a bit further before we lose all light. We will not stay. You will not wish to stay once you understand."

Gunny trotted then sprinted ahead. His tail was alert, ears perked and eyes focused on the hill. Henry had probably been smelling it for a while. With no previous exposure to that particular odor, though, his mind failed to elevate it out of the unconscious.

"What is it, Gunny?" Henry called to the dog's diminishing form.

He hiked his backpack higher on his shoulders and rolled down the sleeves of his sweatshirt. The sun had nearly set in the west, and without its direct light on his skin the air felt much cooler.

"It is amusing what the human mind can do," Ted said.

"How's that?"

"You have seen the hill for miles now. There is not much else to look at, so it steals your eye. You have been predicting a hill for miles, and so that is what your mind sees."

Henry looked from the hill to Ted. "I … don't understand."

"It *is* a hill. That is true. But it is not what you predicted," Ted said, pointing.

Gunny trotted back to him, his head low and ears flat. The dog whimpered and Henry kneeled, preparing to inspect his paws for burrs.

"This is what happened to them. This is what is left."

The sun's light faded to a candle glow. Henry scratched Gunny behind his ears as the dog continued whining. The strange smell breached the surface of his consciousness. Details of the hill, blanks his mind filled in and angles it smoothed over began to reveal themselves.

A pile of bicycles?

No. That did not account for the smell and Ted's cryptic speech.

"We are no longer in love as we once were, for you are no longer our children. Yet we do love you, and this is not how your story should have ended."

Henry's vision narrowed to a vertical slit. Not bicycle seats or handlebars. Elbows and feet. Ted's words blended, settling into a drone Henry no longer understood. He covered his mouth. He was stunned, his mind fighting to blunt the angles, to re-form the hill he *predicted*. There were thousands of corpses and, mercifully, not enough light to reveal them in detail.

Henry's interpretation of the passage of time fluctuated after the world ended. The days were incredibly long, like how summer felt when he was a kid. But his memory of the first week was distorted, the trauma coalesced, compacting smaller and smaller, the gravity of nearly losing Penny to his Stargazer wife warping time.

It seemed like a dream, like the memory of a dream. All those people. Thousands of them walking and dying. The destination unknown and unimportant. He remembered the trails of blood on the asphalt, eventually catching up to the sources. Stargazers grinding their legs to stumps. Walking and walking. Walking to die. Walking to lie down in the west Texas dirt and never rise.

Henry sat, head in hands. Tears spilled, but he did not weep. It was not an adventure. His new life with Penny was not some spontaneous decision to claim a simpler existence. Doc, Lucy, Michael, and Jean were survivors, not gold-hearted vagabonds. The people in the hill before him were dead. Judith was not among them, but there were thousands of Judiths. Thousands of girls just like Penny among those twisted limbs. Millions. Millions of stories that ended mid-sentence.

"We will walk around."

Henry nodded but made no motion to stand.

"Is this what I'm supposed to see? You said it would take five days."

"No. This is not for you. I believe this is for me. For us. For those you called gods. It is what you will learn next. Most gods of your religions are almighty. They know all and see all. This is not possible in the Universe as I understand it. I do not know everything. But it is simple to find a broken tree after a storm and know the wind did it. There are other potentials, but wind is most likely."

Ted extended a hand. Before taking it, Henry said, "Can you answer just one question? I know this all has to happen in some sort of order for it to make sense, but it's the one question we keep asking among ourselves."

"You want to know why them and not you?"

Henry nodded. Ted gestured with his hand and Henry took it.

"When your kind climbed the third step it rippled through the Universe."

"You said it made the spiderweb tremble."

"It did. And your journey did not end there."

Ted's Story, Part Two

To not tire your brain, I will name them the Other. The Other is something that has never lived. It is an observer, not a participant. Now, there are things that have not lived that have the potential for it. A nail is not living, but a nail is made of iron and there is iron in your blood. So, where do you paint the line? Why are you alive and a car is not? Much of your structure is the same. Blood flows through your tubes and gasoline flows through the car. Reproduction? Some humans do not reproduce. Does that mean they do not live?

I am walking off the tracks. My meaning is, the Other had no potential to be a participant on its own. A nail is closer to living. A long time from now, time even as I understand it, your star will explode. The nail will become something else. Maybe part of a living thing. A small chance is still a chance.

What you call 'reality', and I do not like that word but cannot think of one better, is constructed from the same materials. Do you understand?

Henry: No.

Good. The potential for life exists outside of the construction. Do you understand?

Henry: No.

What are those sails children fly? The sails on strings?

Kites! I remembered! A kite is simply wood and paper until it is touched by the wind. When it is touched by the wind it becomes a kite. Life is the same. The potential for life is outside of the construction. It is a choice. But life needs a vessel. What is the wind without grass or trees or kites?

*The Other **had** no potential. It had no choice to make. For a long time, time as you understand it, we were not bothered by the Other. It simply became another color in the background of our world. I do not understand the Other as I understand many things. We do not come from the same place, the same source. Therefore, I must guess at some of it. The Other was not still. There was a wall between us, but it was poking the seams, scraping the mortar.*

We were in love, remember? How did it feel to hold Nickel the first time? Do you remember the color of the walls in that room? Do you remember anything other than her face? We could not see the background of the world was changing. The Other found the weak places.

Finally, it broke through ...

Henry: Are you okay?

I am sorry. We did not notice. There were paths before us that

...

We did not see them. You had made us gods, and it was much more than anything we had been before. We thought we were helping, holding your hands as you mounted the ladder. But that is not a journey to be made with a held hand. You must do it alone, with a full heart and a ready spirit, with love in your tubes and curiosity in your mind. There is no curiosity when it is us who bring the seasons. Your heart cannot be full when there is a secret reservoir for your gods.

I was ... away from here. Across the ocean. I do not recall where the borders you carved begin and end, so I cannot name the land.

There was jungle. There were mountains. It was quite beautiful. I was a god of many names to many people. Most associated me with the tiger. I understood why, but it was not my favorite animal. There were altars in mountain caves, in the meadows between stretches of jungle. They left food and beads. They brought their sick and dying. I loved them. Not with the strength you love Nickel, because they were not children from my body. But I loved them.

One day I came to an altar. The tribe was small, and their offerings were small. They often left shells, feathers, things they found beautiful. I would collect these offerings for a time and return them in ways they did not notice. That day there was something different. I could take many forms then. On that day I was as you see me now.

It was a child. I thought she was sick. Often the old are sick, but there had been children before. She was alone, which I did not like. Where was her father? The jungle is a harmful place, and this child had no guardian. As I neared, I saw she was bound to the altar. A sacrifice? I did not demand such things.

No. Not a sacrifice.

The color faded to the background of our world. Would you notice if there was one new star in your night sky? Would you notice if one brick had been added to your home, or taken away?

I knew this child's name, and so I spoke it. She did not answer. She faced the altar. Her bound hand hung forgotten at her side. Her head tilted west and east. I was looking at her with these same eyes. The same way I look at you now. I had no reason to look in another way.

She turned, this child, and I was prepared for many things. She might have been injured or with fever. I can manage such moments.

I saw the lights in her eyes, and I understood what they were. This child no longer had a name. The name had moved on and become something else. There is more to that story, but I will get to it. The Other had found a way in. The lights in its eyes like, like pennies. Hmmm ... that is interesting to think.

They were brown and gold, but not beautiful. As a god I had little to fear, but I was afraid. It was not simply that the Other had taken the body. What might it achieve with this vessel? It was now a participant in the spiritual migration of its own kind. It was on the ladder.

Life is not simply a body, but there is no life without a vessel. There are moments between. There are moments of dreaming. Do you understand?

Henry: Like hibernation?

That is close. That is very close. And this Other, now hidden within the body of the girl I knew, could not be allowed to climb the ladder, to even access it.

Henry: Did you kill her?

She was already gone, I believed. This was the Other wearing her skin. It looked at her hands, opened and closed the fingers.

*Dream of entering a human form after drifting through the Universe for all of time. Perhaps before time existed in **our** Uni-*

verse. So much darkness, cold you cannot even feel. And then there is sunlight on your skin.

I was a god, but you named us that. The miracles I performed were simply magic tricks, a rearranging of the materials. But I had never interacted with this material before. I called upon the other gods. There were more of us then. Hundreds. Most departed, interested in the trembling of the spiderweb.

Five answered my call and we gathered at the altar. We spoke about what needed to be done. It is simple to stop a heart beating in a chest. It is simple to steal air from the lungs. We could have pulled apart the materials of that body, but the body was not our concern. It was the Other inhabiting the body.

It was night. We each reached inside, not with our hands. With the essence of what you would call a soul. We touched the essence of the Other. It was then I knew the soul of the girl was not gone, not entirely. The Other absorbed part of her. It was not good to touch. I cannot describe it in a way that will make sense for you. I cannot offer you a dream that will compare. It was not good. We each grasped our share of the essence and pulled. The Other, its version of a soul, ripped into six pieces. These we cast in six different directions. If they are not interrupted, they are traveling still, to the edge of the Universe, which will never come. The pieces will simply travel until the end of everything.

I placed the body of the girl on the altar. We covered her in flowers. I mourned for her because, some must die; that is the way of all flesh. But she did not have to. There were many paths before her where this did not happen. What you would call her soul was now a wounded thing, unable to dream, unable to hibernate. Drifting blind.

For a long time, time as you understand it, your ancestor's gods became warriors. Destroyers. Where we found the Other, we cast it into the darkest part of the night sky. There were more like the girl. More people who lost their names, who drifted without dreaming. Now, the color was no longer the background of our world, but the brightest light we could see. We were attuned to it. We hunted it. Exterminated it.

We thought.

Over time, the pieces were smaller and smaller. Harder to find. So small even a god could not sense them.

This is what happened, Henry. This is what happened to your kind. The Other hid inside of you, so small we could not notice. For a long time as you understand time. It learned, in its own way. Those you named gods left, many of them. Those who stayed became less like gods and more like magic people.

Henry: Shamans?

That is like white dog for me. I have known so many names for it I do not have room for new ones. You can keep saying it and I will keep saying it is fine. We served the same purpose, a bridge between people and the unseen world.

You have been under our protection since we came here. Not every god had pure intentions for mankind, but those jesters were restless and did not stay for a long time.

Henry: Time as I understand it?

Yes. We held your hand as you ascended, but we were reaching down to do this. The Universe strives not for ultimate good or evil but balance. Rain is a good thing, but too much of it strips the soil. Sunlight is good, but too much of it turns the rivers to sand. You need rain and light. You need times without rain and darkness. I have told you these words before.

I am walking off the tracks. I will simply say this, we became more human, and our protection was not enough. There must have been a moment where the balance shifted. Where the last of us lost what it meant to be a god. Everything happened so fast.

It did not work as the Other hoped. I do not know if the Other is capable of such a feeling. **You** *are still here. I do not know if that was its plan.*

Henry: But *why* are we still here? What makes us special?

Special is a good word here. You are special. You have moved up the ladder. Not all of you to the same place. But all of you who remain. Still, remember about balance. The ladder must be balanced, too.

Henry held his hands out, the heat from the fire making the skin of his palm feel tight. Every few minutes, he remembered the mound of bodies half a mile behind him and shuddered. Gunny stretched out, a swath of pink belly aimed at the flames. There was peanut butter in the fur of his muzzle, too far for his tongue to reach. Henry managed a single bite of the sandwich, which his stomach at once rejected. Gunny had no qualms.

He had questions for Ted, but Ted was tired of talking.

"We will speak of nicer things in the morning," he said.

"What about the souls of the people who died? What happened to them?" Henry demanded.

Ted shrugged, "It is not the destiny of a soul to simply be human. There are other forms. Here there are no vessels. Dream of the paths before you, not behind. This is what matters. Someday your kind might reach behind to touch those behind paths, but not today."

Henry shook his head as if refusing to let the words settle.

"But–"

"We will speak of nicer things in the morning."

Chapter Twelve

It's About Her

The wind needled through the fabric of Henry's hoodie, goosebumps bubbling over his torso. He had nothing warmer to wear, only thinner layers that would have become uncomfortable without fulfilling their purpose. The summer had been so relentlessly hot he doubted Autumn would ever come. It prodded, casting exploratory fingers. Ted did not notice, or at least he didn't appear to. Henry wondered about his form. Did he feel sensations in the manner of people? He had not traveled the spiderweb in a human body, Henry guessed. It was a curiosity, though, and did not seem worth discussing when so many critical truths went unspoken.

Gunny responded to the drop in temperature by galloping ahead, diminishing until he might have been a piece of lint on a brown cushion.

Though Ted promised to speak of nicer things, he did not appear eager to begin. They walked in silence, the hill of dead hidden behind a slope in the landscape. Henry hoped he would not see it on the way back. His back was stiff, as if expecting a leathery hand to land on his shoulder at any moment.

They walked through campsites long abandoned, town and city folk fleeing murderous or suicidal brethren. There were houses Henry would have explored if given the time, cattle thundering away at their scent. Always, Ted stopped to tear down fences. Henry assisted without thinking about it.

He wondered about Judith's soul. Would he recognize it in a new form? Could everything Judith was fit inside a butterfly? Perhaps size did not matter in these things. More than anything, he wanted to be with Penny again. He felt the invisible tether between them growing taut with each step. Could it sever?

"What was it about us?" Henry said.

They had resumed walking after a break for lunch. Gunny did not race ahead then but trotted slowly, pausing to lick peanut butter from his teeth.

"What do you mean?" Ted said.

"You stayed while the others of your kind, your kind and other kinds, left. You said you fell in love. Why?"

Ted had plucked a plaid long-sleeve from a clothesline. He wore it for a time after complaining about blowing dust. Though the temperature held steady, he removed the shirt then and tied it around his waist.

"That story might speak more of what else moves the spider-web than you."

"You've got a way answering questions without providing any new information."

Ted waggled his fingers.

"Life does not have to be so busy. That's not a good word," he said, motioning with his hands as if trying to pull a better word from the air. "Complicated? That might work. Life is often less complicated. Life with a big L letter. Even your kingdom of animals is remarkable. Much life in other places passes as a ghost. Small as a spark of dust. As complicated as sand. And people are different even more than the kingdom of animals. You would have to grow your understanding of the forms life can take."

"Like what?"

Ted pointed overhead. "You would not say a cloud is living, but there is such life. I have seen it. I have seen life so small a whole civilization could fit in your hand, just as complicated as your kind only very small."

"Why are we different? Why did you not get bored and follow those *jesters* who were interested in the trembling of the web?"

Ted narrowed his gaze. For most of the day he wandered out of conversational range of Henry, punting tumbleweeds and kicking over fenceposts. Ted was never easy to read and his demeanor that day underscored Henry's confusion.

"If you wish for me to say that you are special you can simply ask."

"That's not wha–"

Henry's words were cut short by a suddenly barking Gunny, who bolted with spittle flying.

"Wonder what that's about," Henry said.

"We will see."

Gunny could have been carved from a pillar of salt. His nose aimed to the northeast, the general direction they were headed. Henry thought he was waiting for his companions to catch up, but he did not flinch when Henry called his name.

The paw he used to demand affection or sweep Misfit across the floorboards during one of their play fights stamped the ground. A cloud of dust erupted.

"What is it?" Henry said, rubbing a knuckle against the dog's ear.

The dust settled and a twitching jackrabbit emerged, its back legs angled away from its body. The spine caved in its center, but Henry focused on the eyes. They glowed with amber light, flickering, like a candle sipping the last of its wax.

"It is okay, white dog. You can release it," Ted said.

Gunny obeyed, retreating a few paces though his gaze remained locked on his prey.

Henry scratched the back of his neck, looking from the quivering animal to the miniature wolf.

"Gunny did that?" he said.

Ted nodded, "His grandfathers protected sheep. Now he protects you."

"From that?"

Ted squatted, "It is not a threat. Not yet. The Other gathers, becomes heavier. One day it might become a spider you would notice. That day may not be far now."

"Was it alive?"

Ted crouched over the animal, pinched the fur, rolled it between his fingers. Then he stood and dusted his hands on his jeans.

"Probably. A rabbit is far down the ladder from your kind. There is little for a spirit, and I do not like that word, that would become a rabbit to learn in this world. But it is not off the ladder. Do you understand?"

Henry fought the urge to stomp the rabbit. The lights in its eyes sparked a storm in his belly. What would happen then? Would the light come for him?

Ted made motions with his hands Henry mistook for a signal. His eyes followed the movement, darting to the horizon, but there was only more land aching for the winter to come end its misery. That strange sense of calm, like slipping between freshly laundered sheets, steadied his heart. It was a sense of peace before the chaos. But where were its agents?

The rabbit stood, its twisted paws hovering just beyond the stiffened, yellow grass. Its mouth was limp, bubbly red slaver spilling onto its fur.

"This once was simple," Ted said. Sweat ran in a rivulet down his cheek. "But I am not what I once was, and the Other has become something new."

The rabbit pirouetted, the glow flickering like lightning along the underside of a distant storm. Ted flicked his wrists. The light exited the skull and sailed, a comet streaking into the atmosphere. The rabbit was roadkill, a clump of fur closer to being the ground it rested on than the animal it had been. Gunny yawned and stood, tail sweeping. He moistened his nose with a lick and trotted ahead.

"Where did it go?" Henry asked, eyes directed at the place in the sky where the light disappeared.

"It did not *go*. It is *going*. It will always be."

They spoke of nicer things. The effort to dispel the light changed something within Ted. He side-stepped tumbleweeds rather than kicking them. He rested his forearms on fenceposts rather than dismantling them. His plump fingers plucked the barbed wire but did not seem capable of destroying it.

"Tell me of your life before. It is my favorite thing to know, the lives of people," Ted said.

Henry obliged after clarifying how far back Ted wanted him to go. *The most interesting place.* For Henry, that was when he met Judith. He realized, recalling the story of their romance, he did not remember much of his life before her. It seemed so inconsequential, meaningless. Nothing he did before her had bearing on the person he became. Ted interrupted with questions, points of clarification. He laughed at memories that were not intended to be funny, appeared to fall asleep on his feet when Henry spoke about his father passing.

"Where did he go? In your understanding of reality, what happened to him when he died?"

Ted paused with one hand on his hip. He again wore the shirt he'd stolen from a laundry line, but it could have been made of beetles. He picked at it, scratched his forearms.

"That is not a simple question. The answer must begin with your understanding of life. At what moment does life begin? At what moment does it end? The slime in your pouch," Ted said, pointing to Henry's groin. "Is it alive now?"

"Slime?" Henry asked, fighting a smile. "The *sperm*? I guess I don't know."

"Some believe life is movement. Living things grow, some very slowly. Living things move. Your slime moves. You have other very small things in your body that are alive. No one could claim otherwise. Where does life begin? At a certain age you stop growing, but you are alive. In sleep you do not move, but you are alive. Is it when your heart stops beating?"

Ted began walking again.

Henry said, "I guess scientifically it would be then. Then and when the brain shuts down. I, uh, I've seen it happen up close. The eyes lose focus. Sometimes there's a final breath."

Henry scratched the back of his neck, gritted his teeth to keep the memories from surfacing.

"I am sorry you had to see that. I will share with you my understanding. You are not a body or a mind. You are the captain of a ship. Ships are made of matter, and they will sink, eventually. Every one of them. But you are still a captain, and you are not made of matter."

"Well, what am I made of then?"

Ted gestured to the east, the night sky chasing the setting sun, bleeding its light, "The breath of the Universe."

Henry slept with an arm draped over Gunny. Ted watched over them, as he always did. He, too, was the captain of a ship. He, too, was the breath of the Universe. But he was not the captain he once was, and his time with this ship was nearing its end.

"We will reach it today," Ted said.

There were more hills, more oil derricks. The cattle were just as nervous, stampeding at the scent of them. There were houses that might have been abandoned decades ago, paint flaking free like snakeskin, planks swelling free of their nails.

"Do I get to know what *it* is before we get there?"

"It would be better to see it."

"Why?"

Ted sighed. "Does Nickel treat you this way? Does she ask questions you have already rejected?"

"All the time."

"And what do you say to her?"

"Eventually I give in."

Ted nodded. "Eventually we will be there. I will give in then."

They stopped for lunch as clouds assembled to the north. The temperature had fallen throughout the morning, the wind kicking up dust devils that spun in and out of life like ghosts. Gunny, ever wary, paced as Henry fought through another peanut butter and jelly sandwich. The dog only abandoned his post when his name was called and jerky tossed in his direction.

Henry spoke little, both because of the effort needed to chew Doc's bread and the fact his mind was racing. He sensed what was coming in the way, in another life, he knew there were enemies in the dark even when he could not see them. It was a relic, he assumed, of a long-dead ancestor walking through chest-high grass. The gravity of teeth. If the spiderweb truly touched every grain of sand, every being, maybe it was the connection between them. The silent calculus of a predator weighing the risk of the attack.

Jerky fell out of Gunny's mouth, plummeting to the dirt on a silver bungee cord of saliva. His ears perked, head twitching left and right. He *woofed* low in his throat.

"What is it buddy?" Henry said.

Gunny looked at him, his eyes like wet coals on snow.

"What is it?" Henry asked again.

Gunny *woofed* again and took off.

Henry stood, "Should I be worried?"

The dog flashed white here and there amid the foliage.

"Not right now. We should follow."

Gunny's bark dwindled as the distance between them increased. Then it ceased. The trail was easy to distinguish, paw prints and wisps of white hair like cotton candy in the branches.

"Gunny!" Henry called.

Ted held up a hand, "White dog is just over there. So is the Other. It is heavier. There is more of it. I will do what I am able."

Gunny's growl was like a muscle car idling. There seemed to be no end to it, as if the dog had a limitless supply of oxygen. Henry stepped around a small hill and at first only saw the dog. Gunny faced away from him, his tail alert, shoulders dipped.

"What is—" Henry began, but he saw it then, its fur the same color as the soil. The lights in its eyes. It flashed teeth like daggers. There was a bit of white fur on its muzzle, a smudge of dirt on the crown of its head. Gunny's front right paw hovered in the air, threatening another blow.

"The Other is the captain of this ship. It can access the memories. It is learning how to be a lion," Ted said, then began to twirl his hands. "I am not a god, now. That was your word, not ours."

The mountain lion jolted as if shocked. It retreated a few paces, and Gunny quickly made up that distance. Its tail flicked, glowing eyes searching for the source of its discomfort.

"It is not so simple now."

The cat showed its teeth again, but to no one in particular. It sat on its haunches, eyes blinking rapidly.

"How come we can see it? The lights? Why didn't we see them before?"

Ted nodded but did not answer. His fingers worked as if lathering his hands. The lion's neck stretched, and it stood on its hind legs. It gnashed its teeth, carved the air with its claws. Ted's right hand formed a U. Above it, his left hand mimed grasping a ball. He licked his lips. Sweat beaded across his forehead.

"It's fighting me," Ted whispered.

He wrenched his left hand, and the lion dropped. The light hovered in air, smaller than Henry would have guessed. About the size of a plum.

"I understand. For this there has been only darkness. *You* can see it because it is bigger, and because if you could not see it, you would not be here now. You would have been in the mountain of bodies. *They* could not see it."

Ted brought his hands together and the light flickered in concert.

"I do not have the strength to make it go forever. I can only send it away from here."

He threw his hands and the light followed where his fingers last pointed. Ted dropped to a knee and Henry rushed to him while Gunny inspected the limp predator.

"It is only a bit further now. Look," Ted said.

A faint glow to the northeast, like fire hidden within fog. And something else. Henry's stomach twisted, his muscles twitching in anticipation.

"Let us walk. I may need your help at first."

Before they left Gunny stood over the dead lion and pissed.

Henry's stomach gurgled with each step. Toxic burps singed the back of his throat and coated his tongue with fire. Gunny whined with his nose dusting the ground. He was a ghost of the protector he had been only hours before. His tail was as limp as a rubber hose, and he paused often to look behind, flaring his nostrils as if seeking Jean and Michael's scent on the wind.

Like the pyramid of bodies, Henry did not understand the formation when his eyes distinguished it from the background of rolling hills, mesquite, and dying shrubbery. Without Ted, he would not have understood it even standing in its shadow. They did not come that close.

"We will stop here. White dog has fallen behind and may not rejoin us," Ted said.

"What is it? What am I looking at?" Henry asked.

"The star people built it. It was not their idea to. Like it was not their idea to walk outside and watch the moon. They broke your cities apart, and this is what they did with the pieces. You have in your world the idea of sacred geometry. Do you know it?"

The air was cool but sweat dappled Henry's face. He wiped his mouth with the back of his hand, then bent at the knees and spit.

"It might feel better to be out of you than in you. We will not stay here long. Scared geometry, do you know it?"

Henry stood, pressed a hand to his belly and grimaced.

"I guess so. Like, symbols that mean something to a religion or a culture? There's some special math, too, I think."

"That is close enough. This is the opposite of that. The upside-down of sacred geometry. Your kind uses certain pictures to, how would you say it, purify a message or a space."

"Like the cross?"

"No. That is to remember. This is to rejoin. To communicate."

Henry squinted as to view the structure fully was too confusing for his brain.

"This is a beacon. This formation resonates. It is a beating heart tossed on the spiderweb. Pulsing. It calls to the Other and beyond. I do not know the Other as I know many things. To hold it is the worst feeling I can have in this body. It is not one I seek. It makes me feel less alive," Ted said, then turned his back to the formation. "Do you see the lights? Do you see the colors? They are coming."

Henry could only view it peripherally. He felt like he wanted to rip his skin off, to pluck out his eyes and stomp them into the dirt with the heel of his boot.

"What does it have to do with me, Ted? Why did you take me here?"

Ted grasped Henry's chin and pinned him beneath the weight of his gaze.

"Not you, Henry. Her. It's about her."

CHAPTER THIRTEEN

I Just Wanted to Say Goodbye

One Year Later

"Close your eyes and tell me about the colors you see," Jean said.

Penny obeyed and turned her head this way and that, nostrils flared as if seeking the source of a bad smell.

"I can see Doc. He's in the shed and he's green," Penny said, then adjusted in her seat to face the house. "Dad's in there and he's green but not all the way. There's other colors. Uh, *you* look like a purple, a light purple like an Easter color."

"What else?"

Penny frowned, "I can see them. The bad colors."

"They're not bad. They just are."

Penny crossed her arms over her chest, "Well, what they're doin' is bad. I can see Ted and Vida, kind of. Like maybe what they left behind. It doesn't feel like they're here right now. Nadine is over there. She's sitting on a rock a few miles away. She just sits there, huh?"

"Yes. And what else?"

Penny sighed and slumped in her chair. This was not the afternoon she had planned for herself.

"Michael is upstairs taking a nap. He's like you. Still has some blue in him though. Lucy's in the room next to him listenin' to the radio, but it's not music. She used to be a kind of orange, but now it's red."

"And?"

Penny peeked with one eye.

"And what?"

"Who are you forgetting?"

Penny frowned and sat up. She scanned the yard, the house again, and searched the desert beyond the border of the property.

"You, silly," Jean said.

"Oh! I knew that!" Penny said and closed her eyes again. "I can't really see the color. It's kind of like water, like when the sun hits the water."

"That's close enough," Jean said, and patted Penny's hand.

The girl stood and stretched. Despite the impromptu lesson she was in a good mood. They were going to have a campfire that night. The marshmallows were stale, but they tasted just fine after they'd been toasted. There was a lot of chatter about tonight, conversations that ended when she walked into a room. Something was changing, or about to. She understood that. But before that change there would be s'mores and corn on the cob.

Doc's garden, in its second year, produced more food than they could eat.

"Hey sweetie," Jean said.

Penny wished she had left when she had the chance, "Yes Jean?"

"What color are the dogs?"

Penny knew the answer, but she knew it from memory. She pursed her lips and perched her hands on her hips. Had Henry emerged from the house then he would have recognized the stance as a miniature of Judith.

"Gunny's bright yellow," Penny said, pointing to the yard where the top of his head was just visible above the tall grass. "Like gold."

"And?"

Penny scanned the house.

"Um ..." she said, stepping off the porch. "Misfit?"

Her task forgotten, she walked forward and framed her mouth with her hands. She shouted the dog's name and then listened for the tinkling bell on her collar.

Penny's voice was gone. She had shouted for hours. She sat in silence around the campfire that night, one marshmallow after another blackening to coals as she stared beyond the flames. If Misfit was there, she would have seen her, bright yellow like Gunny. The voices around her sounded like a vacuum cleaner.

How could they talk when Misfit was missing? Yes, she had gone exploring before, but never without Gunny, and she always returned before dark.

There were lights in the sky. There always were, like stars slowly falling. But they were not beautiful. Jean, her dad, and even Ted attempted to explain them to her, and she nodded and smiled without really paying attention.

Decisions were made. Penny did not know what they were. She went to bed early and pretended to be asleep when her dad tiptoed into the room. His breaths settled into a sleep pattern, and Penny eased out of bed like a mouse sneaking past a napping cat.

She stood at the edge of the yard, at the border where the grass grew wild. She waited there, knowing she was supposed to be there but not knowing why. She called to Misfit, but not with her voice. She called to her with her heart. She called and waited, the Universe above her, some stars falling others staying in place.

"Misfit?" Penny whispered, kneeling.

The grass parted, and the dog's familiar face peeked through.

The tears came. Not from joy. She understood Misfit's fate despite her hours of searching, of shouting until her throat hurt like she'd swallowed a cactus. Some part of her understood it. Jean talked about *paths* and Penny nodded and smiled without really paying attention. There was a path with Penny and Misfit together, and a fork where Penny's kept going.

The dog showed its little white teeth. The lights in its eyes were an ugly yellow, closer to brown. This thing was not Misfit, Penny understood. She'd seen Ted and Vida perform their magic tricks many times.

"Get out of her," Penny growled through clenched teeth.

She held up her hands as Ted did. She didn't know *how* he did it. She only knew she wanted what had taken over her dog to be gone. Not just gone. She wanted it to not exist. Ted and Vida sent the lights away, sometimes far away. But there was not a far *enough*.

Penny closed her left hand into a fist. She felt its shape, the throb of its essence. The lights in Misfit's eyes flickered, the limbs spasming.

The edge of the Universe was not far enough.

She clapped them together, tears spilling onto the knot of her hands. Penny squeezed her eyes closed, but she heard Misfit's body crumbling.

"I'm so sorry," she whispered.

In real time, she stood there for only a minute. In time as she understood it, she stood there for an eternity.

When she opened her eyes, the light was gone, and Misfit lay on the grass as if she was only napping. This was not true. There was no Misfit. There was only the house she used to live in.

Penny wiped snot from her nose and then looked at her hands. She looked to the stars. The light was gone. It was not traveling to the edge of the Universe. It was gone.

She sat in Jean's rocking chair, Gunny beside her. She tried to pet him, but he had so much fur he probably didn't feel it. On the table to her left there was a shoebox, its lid taped shut. Penny understood many things without having the words to explain them. She mirrored Ted in that way. She continued calling to Misfit, feeling their connection frayed but not severed.

Penny called with her heart, with some place inside her that felt like her heart. Gunny sensed it first. He scrambled to his feet, both ears perked and aimed forward.

"There you are," Penny whispered. "It's okay."

The light was bright yellow, almost gold. She knew it at once, knew its warmth.

"I just wanted to say goodbye."

And she did, for hours, until the sun rose. Then like blowing a dandelion, she sent the light away to become something else.

———

After the funeral, Penny diverted her attention to Gunny. Her eyes still red from crying, she stood before him and pointed at the ground, a homemade dog biscuit behind her back.

"Sit Gunny," she said.

Gunny obeyed. It was the one command he had mastered.

"Down Gunny."

Penny motioned to the ground with a flattened hand. Gunny blinked and held a paw up.

"No. Down Gunny."

Gunny prodded her with the paw, his brows furrowed in confusion.

Henry and Doc shared the bench overlooking the memorial site. They'd added new stones for relatives turned Stargazers. They installed the marker for Michael's mother on what would have been her fiftieth birthday.

"I don't think those are the trainin' sort of dogs," Doc said, nodding at Gunny, whose paw rested on Penny's thigh.

"Kind of like a cat, you know. Like I can sense a million thoughts going on in his mind, but the only tool he has to express himself is that damned paw," Henry said.

"Good protector, though."

"You got that right. You should have seen him face off with the mountain lion. I know the, uh, lion was infected, so to speak, but I would have given Gunny better than fifty-fifty odds. You said they were bred to fend off wolf attacks, right?"

"That's what I recall. A lion is a different ball game. They typically don't start a fight they don't think they can win."

Henry dusted his hands on his jeans and stood. "I'm glad he was there."

"You'll be taking him, then?"

Henry nodded. "Want to give Penny a few days. She's taking this really well, but I don't think she was fully present for last night's discussion. Might not understand the plan."

"I can't say I understand it. Ted has a way of speaking that makes me feel like I'm dreamin' while I'm wide awake."

"Well, to put it simply, she needs more experience. Needs more exposure if she's ever gonna learn."

"Learn what, Henry?"

"How to become a god."

Apocalypse Radio

The Stargazers were weak, but you are not. The Stargazers were not worthy, but you are. I do not know how much of my audience remains, who is still listening. I have been gone for some time.

Gone. That is a funny word. It makes it seem like I was just over there, somewhere. Like I was just beyond the horizon. I went much further than that, further than I knew I could travel. The memories from before are clouded, like they were someone else's life. I do recall seeing the monument for the first time. I remember the lights swarming around it. I did not know what they were, only that they were wonderful, and I wanted to be closer.

I've never felt God inside of me, the Holy Spirit or anything like it. I've never had a religious experience. I've never wanted one. Old books and a non-scientific understanding of the world. Why would I want that? Religion is an anchor not a tool. It keeps you from straying, from seeing beyond the confines of its patchwork construction.

I wanted this, not fully understanding what *it* was. I wanted to be near it, to feel it. My last clear memory is abandoning my comrades to run toward the monument, to embrace the light as if it was God raining down.

I nearly died. Part of me did. Part of me hid within my body, emerging days or weeks later emaciated and no longer in full possession of myself. I was hungry, but not alone. I learned to walk again. *We* learned to walk ... together. As one.

We traveled so far, in the world and within our now shared spirit. We found our way back to you to bring you this message.

Let the light in.

Let the light in.

You are worthy.

Do not turn away from this gift. It is inside you already. There are others like us, others who embraced the light. There will be more. You will see us soon.

We are coming.

Quick Favor

T hank you so much for dedicating your time to reading this book! May we ask a quick favor?

Will you please take a moment to leave a review on Amazon, Goodreads, or wherever you purchased the book? Your words have power. Your review can help this book reach more readers. We appreciate you!

Acknowledgements

I have to begin with my daughter, Magnolia, who said, "I wonder what happened to Jean?" in response to my ruminating about what to write next a couple years ago. I began to wonder what happened to her as well. I went to sleep thinking about Jean, Henry, and Penny. I think it is the mark of a good story, or maybe good characters within a story. You don't forget about them when you close the book. They've become a part of you.

Magnolia was not alone in wondering what happened next. I fielded many guesses as to what the Stargazers phenomenon actually was. Honestly, I hadn't decided for myself when I finished the novella. I told the story I wanted to tell and left the why up to the reader. I hope Ted and his ilk, as well as the Other, are at the very least interesting to those who enjoyed the mystery of the Stargazers.

Somewhere between dreaming and wondering, I began writing. I kept a somewhat narrow focus on this story, the direct sequel to Stargazers. There is a larger world outside of these characters, though, and I am excited to share what I've come up with. A few years ago, as I was in the process of writing Skylights,

I asked on social media if it was possible for a story to expand beyond its original genre. Thankfully, it is, as I was made aware of several examples. The next entry in the Skylights Universe is titled The Ranger. The story is plotted. Now I just need to write the damn thing.

Thank you to Magnolia. Thank you to Miranda, who always helps me find facets to characters that were hidden from me. Thank you to Celso Hurtado for reading this entire novel, my first published novel-length work, and telling me it was good. Thank you, Lucas, for making me feel bad about head hopping but good about my prose. Thanks to Chris Panatier for creating the cover art image based on a much poorer rendition I sent him. Thanks to Geoff for helping us make cover art into a cover. Thanks to Becky LeJeune who I did not consult when deciding to publish this through my own (co-owned) press. Thanks to Sobelo Books! And thanks to Joe at Cemetery Gates and Sadie for giving Stargazers to the world.

Finally, thank you to the readers who let me know what I do is meaningful.

About L.P. Hernandez

L.P. Hernandez writes horror and speculative fiction, including the hit short story collection, *No Gods, Only Chaos*. You can find his short stories on The NoSleep Podcast and in anthologies from Cemetery Gates Media, Sinister Smile Press, and Dark Matter Magazine. When he's not writing, he serves as a Medical Service Corps officer in the U.S. Air Force. He loves heavy metal, using cruise control to save gas, his wife and kids, dogs of all sizes, and a crisp high five.

More great titles from Sobelo Books
available at www.SobeloBooks.com
and wherever books are sold.

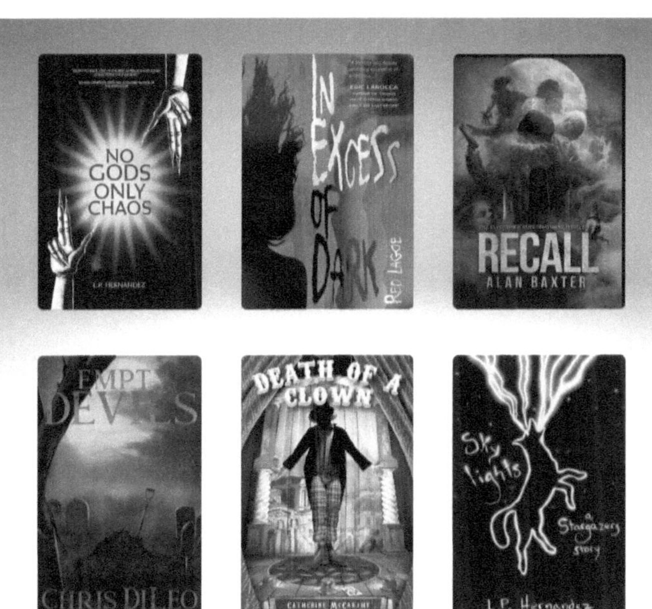

www.ingramcontent.com/pod-product-compliance
Lightning Source LLC
Chambersburg PA
CBHW031033310726
48969CB00007B/1964